LARRY FRANCIS

I0617795

HALVES

Time & Place Prize Publishing

Chicago

ISBN – 13: 978-0-61-575679-0

A Time & Place Prize Publication

For Laura

HALVES

WHAT DO I THINK? Okay, I think you're a fucking moron for asking, that's what I think. But the real issue isn't that you asked. The real issue is why. And, particularly, why now? A little late, don't you think? What could you possibly do with such information? You know you won't listen anyway, you feculent cretin. You appear incapable. You want to do things your way. You think you already have all the answers. Oh Jesus, don't scrunch your face like that, it only makes you more grotesque. And don't turn away from me. Be a man for Christ's sake. Okay. Okay. Shut the fuck up. I don't even want to hear you breathe. Let's see how well you pay attention. And I'll try to put it into language you can understand.

Life

It's all we know, isn't it? If it weren't for life we wouldn't be here and we wouldn't be having this inane discussion. Life is our one and only point of reference. We believe we are alive and we treat everything else that moves or breathes or breeds as being alive too. It's a cosmic accident perpetuated blindly, unthinkingly, no more, no less. Although we know that everything, every goddamned thing in the whole universe and beyond, is made of the same unseen building blocks whirring and spinning and colliding and interacting, our hubris impels us to differentiate between living and non-living, to construct a spectrum to which we pin values and morals. I am more important than you (the ultimate axiom). Americans are more important than Africans. Dolphins are more important than earthworms. Bullshit. We construct this imaginary hierarchy of life: my neighbor's Shih Tzu pissing on my lawn is alive but the sun raining neutrinos isn't. For all we know we aren't any more alive than Mt. Rushmore or a piece of driftwood or the Crab nebula. We are simply at varying stages of entropy. Life doesn't allow perspective. It mandates and codifies illusion. Its definition is transience.

What does it mean to live a good life? How the fuck would I know? I don't think it matters one iota. It's a game we play with ourselves, conveniently changing the rules whenever we wish. Boy, that Buddha really knew what it meant to live. Oh no, Donald Trump has it all figured out. What about George Clooney? That's the way to live, all right. Pick one. Pick none. It doesn't matter. It'll pick you . . . or it won't. You wouldn't know the difference. And in your tiny, belabored mind you will think that life is precisely as it should be. What a crock!

Marriage

I'm sure to some homely, boring motherfucker this seemed like a good idea at the time. The incredible thing is that the rest of us bought into it. Yeah, let's pledge our undying fidelity to one another for eternity. For Christ's sake we struggle to commit to a cell phone plan. Yet we have no difficulty promising another person we will be faithful for the remainder of our miserable lives. And miserable we will be. It's just not in our nature. Listen, I get the argument that a stable home life is beneficial to children, yadda, yadda, yadda. But you can't tell me that marriage is about what's good for children. And you can't tell me it's about love, whatever the fuck that is. As a species we fared for a long time without this punitive institution. Then, almost overnight, it became almost compulsory. No one can convince me that this isn't merely an extension of economics, that money isn't behind it all. Marriage has always been more about finance than feelings. Some-one, somewhere, somehow, managed to invert this and get us to believe that marriage is the only answer in a doomed grail quest for happiness in human sexual relationships.

Here's a little marriage poem for you: Marriage is for temerarious halfwits/Another layer of shit we willingly slather on/Till one day we awaken to find ourselves entombed/In our own inspissated feces.

Now that's an epithalamium I can get behind, one with some grit, some truth.

Work

Talk about the shit we've bought into. Work is worse than marriage. At least the marriage covenant implies sex. Work flips the contract over and fucks you. To see the multitudes pouring into office buildings, zigzagging their way toward cubicles like rats in a maze makes my skin crawl. And if that weren't enough we then spend the rest of the day doing meaningless shit with meaningless people so that we can earn enough money to do something meaningful with the sliver of time we have left. How ass backwards is this? We are actually raising our buttocks begging to be buggered. I mean most rot away staring at a computer screen so they can better enjoy the few minutes remaining after they've just wasted the bulk of their day. Are we really this pea-brained?

And to those who say they like their job (there are even those who will claim to love their job) all I can say is that you are even more moronic than the rest of us. At least we know we are stupid. Most of these idiots aren't even clever enough to realize how awful they have it. If I felt any pity for other people this is where I might. Poor bastards.

Now don't get me wrong. I understand that we have to work. I mean we couldn't survive without food, shelter, etc. So I'm not anti-work per se. But there is a colossal breach, a yawning fucking chasm, between working to fulfill our needs and moiling away our lives because that's what everyone else does. Sure the world needs drudges, I guess, but I'll be goddamned if I volunteer for the job.

You don't believe me, do you? You think because I have, or rather had, my own business that I don't know what I'm talking about. Well, let me tell you something. Starting your own company is more work than anything. Yes, being the boss is better than being a drone. But unless you are really disciplined, really resolute, your company becomes your life and you lose sight of everything else. Life becomes business, the lines blur, and you lose yourself forever. The only way out of this is to start your own enterprise, work your butt off until it's successful and sell it. Then go and live life. Or better yet just inherit enough and take work out of the equation entirely.

Children

I cannot overestimate the danger here. These little fucks embody the most insidious evil you will ever face. They go from helpless, shrieking, shitpissvomit blobs to helpless, shrieking, hormone-driven psychopaths before finally, thanklessly, leaving to terrorize someone else. Children are midget incubi and succubi. Raising a child is a form of voluntary leprosy. You watch yourself deteriorate, see your nose fall off your face because you haven't slept in a decade, a patchwork of veteran lesions holds you together as paralysis slowly eases the struggle. So why do people do it? So you can feel better about yourself? So you can pretend that your life had meaning? Some fucked-up bid for immortality? Stupid cunts. More likely, given our incredible short-sightedness and idiocy, it comes down to the fact that despite the ubiquity of birth control we are still too stupid to protect our independence and control our sexual impulses. Anyone who thinks having children will make their life better earns automatic and immediate induction into the pinhead hall of fame. Trust me it will make your life worse, much worse. True, it will no longer be your sad, pathetic life. It will be your sad, pathetic life in service of another sad, pathetic life. And the cycle goes on. I guess in a way it makes sense. Procreating is really the only thing we have been consistently good at. If we had any balls at all men would castrate themselves and women would stich up their vaginas.

Religion

Really?!?! Do I really have to say anything about this? I think religion for most people is the only way they can endure children. How's that?

I've never understood this need to believe in a God. I mean intellectually I get the fact that it's awfully scary to be alone in this world. I do. But to create your own invisible protector(s) and yearn for an imaginary afterlife? I mean that's some crazy shit. Are we still that frightened? Have we learned nothing in the last 50,000 years? Yet it persists . . . like body hair. And if one more lobotomized motherfucker says to me 'you'll never understand, it's all about faith' I'm going to gut him with an izmel. Faith, you morons, is just as imaginary as your fucking savior. Using one to explain the other doesn't prove a goddamned thing.

Here's an idea for Disney or maybe FOX. Create a cartoon that pits all the Gods and Goddesses ever imagined against one another in weekly competition. It would be years before you exhausted the supply. A computer program would mete out the blow by blow fight based on their presumed powers. In one episode you could have Astarte face off against Hermes, the winner to battle Ganesha. Next could be Anubis versus Tezcatlipoca. I doubt that Jesus Christ with his paltry miracles and card tricks would fare very well against Loki or Neptune, but we'd have to wait and see, wouldn't we? And, in the end, we would all agree to beseech and serve whichever God or Goddess won the cartoon competition . . . at least until the new season begins. Now that's religion the American way. . . to the victor go the kneels.

Whether or not religion has done/does/will do more good than bad is beside the point. Jesus, consider all the time and effort spent designing, creating, modifying, editing, supporting, refining, updating, proselytizing, and enforcing all the religions we've ever had on this planet. And now imagine if we'd spent it in some other way. Don't you think we just might be better off or that we may have found more productive ways to spend all that time and energy? Debating how

7

many angels fit on the head of a pin or whether women should wear a burka strikes me, at the very least, as not the most productive way to spend our miserable lives on this planet.

Consciousness

This is a tricky topic so pay attention. I don't want you branding me a solipsist or arguing that I've made some kind of category mistake. It would defeat the purpose of this entire exercise. So listen the fuck up.

Consciousness is an illusion. Look how simple that is. Consciousness is not real. It does not exist. We have duped ourselves. What most people call consciousness is a perpetuated misunderstanding going back to Descartes. Some geniuses bought into his dualism concept and *voilà* a few centuries later everyone believes there's a contradistinction between your mind and your body. What a load of crap! And a relatively recent load of crap at that. You want another word for consciousness? It's focus. That's all it is. Focus. You (for lack of a better term) attend to things and then think that you (the pronoun in this context makes me cringe) are willing/controlling this 'thought' process. You (I am at the mercy of language's limitations) believe that you (whatever that means) are in charge. Your belief in a consciousness is just that, a belief, a feeling, the same kind of belief/feeling people report when they 'know' they saw a UFO or were abducted by aliens. Bullshit!

I see you shaking your head, you ignorant pustule.

Yes, I know your mother has faith, doesn't she? Here. I'll prove it to you. Every time you think you make a conscious decision to act—every single fucking time!—your brain starts the act half a second before you 'decide' to act. Read Libet if you don't believe me. Furthermore, everything we experience, everything we 'think' we've 'sensed,' has already been experienced and processed by our brains *before* we are 'conscious' of it. It's already happened. Our entire existence is on a half second time delay. Consciousness is merely belated context. It's a shadow play. This is all science, you dumb shit, not belief or wish or hope. It's science. It's apodictic. Just accept it and move on. Besides, life is really more fun when you're not conscious of it. If this is too much for you then think of consciousness as a tool, nothing more. Like a hammer, it can be used to build wonderful things. On the other hand, it can also be used to bludgeon your neighbor to death. I'll stick with illusion, thank you very much.

The Planet

It's truly an amazing and wonderful accident that our goldilocks planet managed to spawn all it has: blue seas and skies, green rainforests and white mountain tops. When you begin to add up all the billions and billions of galaxies it becomes less astonishing, but still it's quite remarkable. What a shame that we appear in a mad rush to destroy it. Yet, despite our best efforts to the contrary, I think that the planet may be more resilient than we realize. As a species we may not survive our rape of the Earth, but I like to think that the planet itself has a few tricks left. I know the smart money is on the increasingly rapid flaying of our orb; however, I hold out hope that nature will exact her revenge ridding herself of our nuisance long before we've managed to kill the host. My bet is on plague or pestilence, that sort of thing. Of course once the sun begins its curtain call in a few billion years then even our once glorious planet must accept the inevitable.

People

Tall, smelly children lacking the excuse of youth. Given how fucked up we are it's beyond belief, imperfect brain aside, that we've become the dominant species on the globe. At the slightest provocation we try to destroy one another and yet here we are. Perhaps our weapons simply are not advanced enough . . . yet.

I know you're well aware of my utter disdain for people. Despite our relatively brief time together, it has been on display. I haven't worked up the sufficient amount of bile to go into definitive detail and buttress my contempt. Suffice it to say that human beings are: ignorant, lazy, coarse, abhorrent, short-sided, hostile, intractable, malodorous, egomaniacal, monomaniacal, cruel, selfish, greedy, churlish, ugly, fearful, bitter, ham-fisted, pompous, cloying, deviant, pedantic, equivocal, dyspeptic, fat, ridiculous, thoughtless, pleonastic, deceitful, unexceptional, prejudiced, fickle, wretched, baleful, ill-mannered, pedestrian, flaccid, insolent, capricious creatures. I could go on like this for days, but even you get the point, right? And believe me I am being kind. We are much, much worse than this truncated, dispassionate list of words would lead you to believe.

Now I would admit that human beings can, at times, be attractive, wonderful to one another and even achieve the magnificent. But these events are so rare I categorize them as statistical anomalies and don't see that they hold much value or promise for our species.

Technology

This is our double-edged sword, isn't it? If Mother Nature doesn't destroy us, we'll do it ourselves in our reckless drive for advancement. Don't get me wrong. I think technological advancement is, apart from our procreating prowess, our greatest accomplishment. It's just that we are so obtuse (add this to our list above) we fail to realize the liabilities of our advances. And one day this will probably lead to our demise. Live by the machine, die by the machine, I guess.

You are probably nodding your head in agreement because you are imagining a nuclear holocaust destroying us all. But you don't have to get all Armageddon to conceptualize technology's insidious hold on us. Christ, before this mess, wherever you went you'd see them with the wires hanging from their heads, the electronic buds plugged into their ears, tapping out text messages to one another, loser to loser. To an extent we haven't considered, we have already made technology such a normal extension of ourselves we wouldn't know what to do without it. Try taking a kid's Game Boy away or a teenager's iPhone and see what happens. By the time you're my age you'll probably have some freakish nano-bots coursing through your body in an unwise attempt to make everyone live longer. At the very least your children will have GPS microchips implanted so you don't lose the little fuckers. The merger of man and machine cannot be stopped, at least not by fools like us. So, slowly, we will all turn into machines, a transition of our own making, eagerly ceding our humanness to our perceived ingenuity all in a misguided attempt to make things better for the eight decades we reign on this planet. Good luck with that. My only solace is that I'll be long dead before you people start to honestly consider living forever. What an unimaginable hell that would be!

Drugs

Here's the thing about drugs: we have no idea what we are talking about. If you ever wanted an illustration of our inanity as a species this is it. Let me ask you, what's a drug? Your first response would be something like, 'well, what do you mean by drug?' And that's precisely my point. We have no fucking idea what we are talking about! Are drugs legal or illegal, controlled or over-the-counter? Is caffeine a drug? What about nicotine? Or cocaine, marijuana or ephedrine? LSD was once legal, now it's not. So was cocaine. Nicotine is currently legal but I don't think anyone would give you very good odds that this will always be the case. You've got millions of torpulent, qat-chewing people all over the world lawfully rotting their teeth? Yet others go to prison for smoking a joint? See, we have no idea what we are doing. It's impossible to control something when you don't know what you are trying to control. If the goal is to control everything that we might ingest that is bad for us, then where is the law banning high fructose corn syrup, soda or tequila? And, by the way, I've seen people get high just as easily off a chocolate mousse as a Valium.

Everything we ingest has an effect on us. Every goddamned thing. Most of the time we don't notice the side effects, sometimes we do. But for some depraved reason our omniscient society feels it must regulate those consumables providing the most pleasant side effects. Well it's a slippery slope. So don't come crying to me when your enlightened legislature outlaws lollipops or seeks to control mango consumption.

People will always find a way to help themselves feel better . . . no matter what the ultimate price. You know why? Because life is painful. Life hurts. Disaster or not, life is cruel. And, if some of these unfortunate fucks want to feel a little less pain, who are you to say they can't? Who are you to dictate how someone should live their life?

Politics, Sports and other Entertainment

It's no wonder that we spend most of our wretched, adult lives discussing one of these three topics. They are all about competition and competition is what human beings are all about. We are social competitors. And it's all about winning. Let me take that back. Sometimes it's also about the valiant fight. Occasionally we enshrine those who fall short in the face of long odds. But mostly it is about winning.

Rarely does history remember the losers of political campaigns or bowl games or American Idol. No, we deify our winners. We strive with the winners, exalt with them, revel in our shared humanity and then we ferret around for every last little detail about them so we can pick endlessly, exposing every blemish in an effort to feel better about ourselves, so we can pretend *we* are not losers. Almost instantly it becomes about *hamartia*. It's an interesting dynamic we've embraced. We do our utmost to share in their brief moment of triumph, a scintillating few seconds of victory, which unites us all as human beings. And as soon as the glow of glory fades (votes have barely been tallied, trophies are still burnished) we turn on them. We put the winners on pedestals only to kick the stands away once the emotion of the competition has waned.

Whether of political victors, sports heroes or entertainment icons, our favorite pastime is criticism. And the key psychological impetus behind this criticism is, lo and behold, our own bell curve mediocrity. If someone is better than us at something then they must be worse than us at something else and we should shout this from the rooftops. We are truly a petty species.

Food

I shan't share much of my utter disgust with those repulsive fucks who lurch around with one chubby hand in a bottomless bag of Cheetos while the other clutches a 32-ounce Mr. Pibb. And then they have the temerity to seek sympathy for their 'condition'. I don't give a rat's fat ass. Just don't sit next to me on a plane or wipe your greasy hands on anything other than your parachute-sized shirt. You want to be fat, go ahead. I don't care. But don't ask me to respect you for it.

Food for me is either something to be savored—something prepared by an expert to appeal to all of my senses: an epicurean experience—or it is simply fuel to keep trudging through this miserable existence. That's it. It's either something to appreciate or a chore. There is no in-between. Obviously, unless you happen to be king, sybaritic culinary events are few and far between. Thus food, and the process of eating to live, is more work than anything else. It's like if you were forced to consciously inhale every time your body needed to breathe, except there is all this preparation attached. What would you like to eat? Or more often, what do you feel like? And the answer is invariably, 'I don't care.' So unless we are off to one of those rare orgies of gormandism, let's just get something quickly so I have the requisite energy to survive for another six hours until I have to contemplate this miserable chore once again.

And then we have the *coup de grace*: to eat with others. I understand that sharing a meal is supposed to be one of those quintessential human activities of paramount import to our species, but quite frankly, other than engaging in group defecation or visiting a vomitorium, I can't think of a more unappetizing spectacle. Manners aside, a shared meal is a melee of partially masticated foodstuff flying in all directions amidst a cacophony of smacking lips, gastro-intestinal eructions and garrulousness complemented by revoltingly awkward facial contortions. *Bon appetit!*

War

War?!? Still!?! It's incredible to me! Are we that fucking stupid? Look, I understand anger and I get the quest for power and all that, but by now war should be the musty stuff of history. People should study the phenomena in school and think 'what ignoramuses those people were.' To know that in this day and age anyone would willingly sacrifice his (or her) life because someone else, someone well-protected and comfortable mind you, orders them to absolutely stupefies me. I don't give a shit what kind of jingoistic, revenge-mongering lies these brainwashed bastards have been exposed to; the methods don't matter to me. But the fact that human beings are willing to travel hundreds or thousands of miles to kill absolute strangers is mind-numbing. You know what, if you are attacked, if someone physically attacks you or your family, go nuts!! Become an animal! Beat that guy or gal to death with your bare hands! It's your right. It's self-defense. But to go to war!? To 'declare' war. Who was the fucking shyster who first tried to civilize war by 'declaring' it? Some obese asshole somewhere sat in a room and said, 'you know what? If we put a façade of gentility on this whole war thing it'll be an easier sell to all those stupid fuckers out there. So let's pretend to be diplomatic about it. Let's pretend we've done everything we can to avoid this. Let's tell them that there is no alternative. Let's say we've exhausted all other possibilities. Duty calls. Your country needs you.' That Henry the Fifth shit sounds good pouring from the pen of Shakespeare, doesn't it? But there isn't much poetry in the rape of an 11 year-old girl or the castration of a father in front of his children or picking pieces of your grandmother's flesh from your face after your apartment has been shattered by a missile. There's your real war. War is horrific. War is sickening. War destroys. There is no such thing as a good war. Defend yourself, yes. But don't you ever tell me that there isn't another option, that there is no alternative. There is always an alternative.

Oh, and another thing, stop using the word war so flippantly. That might be part of the problem, one of the reasons the sheep don't fear the word. War should be reserved for clans killing clans, be they nations,

17

tribes, neighbors, families, etc. There is no war on terrorists. There cannot be a war on drugs. You can't have a war against obesity or poverty. Go ahead, you stupid fucks, fight these things to be sure. Arrest terrorists, stop the import of drugs, help people lose weight or find jobs, but don't call it war. Find another word, it doesn't sound nearly as good as you think it does in sound bites.

Weather

Too soon? Too bad. Talk about the weather. Whether it rains or not is none of my concern. Get it. Whether-weather. It's a joke pin-head. No, it's not, it's funny. I read an article not too long ago that claimed the British spent 60% of their time talking about the weather. The implication was that most of this time was spent complaining about the weather, but that's another story. Imagine if it's true and we spend so much of our precious time on something that, more than most things, is meaningless. Sure thousands of years ago weather meant drought and death, the recent present being a statistical anomaly, a fluke. But can't we get past that? Do you think our forebears spent more or less time than we do discussing the weather? I can tell you this—they didn't have as much time devoted to it in their newscasts, that's for certain. My God, the charts and maps, the radar, weird squiggly lines, occluded fronts, cloud heights, simulated lightening strikes, etc. It's all a little too much, don't you think? And then they're still wrong most of the time anyway. Extra, extra! Hot in summer! Cold in winter! Surprise, fucking, surprise. It's going to be what it's going to be. Deal with it. And if we really need to talk about it so goddamned much, maybe we should learn how to change it. Don't like the weather, then move. But don't be surprised to find weather there too. Dumbfucks.

Advertising

One day people are going to look back on advertising and say, 'to think we were actually paying companies to make us miserable'. It'll make the cigarette companies look like charities.

I believe in the depths of my imaginary soul that advertising is one of the greatest evils on our planet. It's such an insidious, pernicious, repugnant enterprise that it literally makes me ill even thinking about it. Wake up, you stupid fucks!!! It's all just an institutionalized con game, inducing lemmings to buy things they don't need and can't afford. Come on you miserable bastard, spend half your disposable income on a Mercedes-Benz so you can feel superior to your neighbors. Hey, you feckless cuckold, you know your wife won't sleep with you unless you get her diamonds from Jared. Trust me, absent parent, your children will delight in these playful sea monkeys. Bullshit! Though it is interesting that these things we don't need and can't afford would be exponentially less expensive if the producers of such dross didn't pray at the altar of the advertising

19

companies and their salvation armies of focus groups and market research experts. Find one shred of nobility in the 'art' of marketing, I defy you. And don't give me the bullshit that they are only giving people what they want or that these products can really improve a consumer's quality of life. That's fucked up, rationalized cant. First of all people don't know what they want until they are told . . . by advertisers. Secondly, if you actually believe such crap you've already consumed too much Kool-Aid to ever be rehabilitated, to ever hope for redemption.

Still for all its evil I can't help but accept that advertising is somehow part of our very fiber as a species. It is endemic. After all, what are smiles or blond hair but advertisements. Isn't every interaction, each time we try to put our best foot forward, simply an attempt to promote our own insecure worth? Aren't we all just scrambling blindly on an enormous ant-heap trying to impress one another?

Fear

I'm afraid to tell you about this. Just kidding, you stupid fuck. Fear may have had its place thousands of years ago, but now all it does is seriously mess us up. Yes, even now. What is everyone so afraid of? Jesus Christ, you'd think their lives were so goddamned wonderful that they couldn't afford to have their bliss interrupted even for a second. Relax people; take a breath. The simple fact is that our fears, all of them, result from a

misinterpretation of bodily processes. You see sometimes the sympathetic nervous system is activated by an
increase in the rate of noradrenergic activity in the locus
coeruleus while similarly experiencing an abundance of
catecholamines at neuroreceptor sites. In other words
hyperarousal occurs, or, if you prefer, the fight or flight
response or acute stress response is triggered. However
you choose to label it, the reality is that we are afraid
because our bodies signal us to be afraid. Now that's all
well and good if you happen to be Australopithecus or
a hit man, but most of us in the twenty-first century
don't need to fight or flee. So we conjure up involved
tales of neuroses and phobias to help us explain and
understand our physiology. We complain of ailuro-
phobia, algophobia, dromophobia, haptephobia, muso-
phobia, ophidiophobia, taphephobia, toxicophobia and
hundreds of others. We are afraid to fly, we are afraid
of the dark, we are afraid of commitment, we are afraid
of germs, we are afraid of water, we are afraid of dying
young, we are afraid of getting old, we are afraid of
being alone, we are afraid of one another. We are afraid.

The bottom line is that fear has become a
condition rather than the response our genetic
evolution intended. So all you fearful motherfuckers
out there listen up: the only thing you really have to fear
is death . . . the rest is just mental masturbation. And, in
the event it escaped you, we are all going to die anyway
so why waste your little time fearing the imaginary or
the inevitable?

IN THE BEGINNING THERE was the rain.

And good and evil flowed forth.

They roused to the sound of rainfall slowly, fitfully, in small numbers at first, the round clear drops cleansing broad green leaves and burnishing black bark, transforming their surroundings into a glistening, unrecognizable, new world of dampness and danger. Beasts great and small sloshed and screeched with purpose, their tracks and noise disappearing into the ooze, their odors purged. Deafening and relentless, the rain sought no less than total dominion. Huddled in the deepest recess of a rock-shelter, the only home they'd known for a thousand generations, the feeble light of a pitiful fire revealing petrified faces, the clan cowered awaiting the inevitable. The rain would never stop. They were alone. They had been abandoned. They would die.

The gods had not spoken since the rains began.

The gods who controlled night and day;
The gods who directed them where, what and how to hunt;
The gods who taught them to tame fire;
The gods who told them with whom to couple;
The gods who carved the rock they called home;
The gods who protected them from plant and animal;
The gods who talked to their ancestors;
The gods . . . were silent.

Day after day, night after night, they pressed against one another in lamentation while slowly exhausting their rotting scraps of food, the fire burning the last of its fuel. The rain drummed on. Nothing was spared the wrath of the rising water. As they prepared for death, one of them spoke up. I have heard from the gods, he exclaimed. They have not abandoned us. They are still here. They are with us. They still love us. And they will always protect us, he said. Confused, yet hopeful, the others asked, why do they only talk to you? Why do they no longer speak to us? Why have they altered our world? What do they ask of us? They have yet to tell me, he replied. But let us turn our lamentations into prayer and sacrifice. This will summon them . . . back to me.

And the clan did what they were told. And on the morrow the chosen one reported: The gods have witnessed our sacrifice and heard our prayers. Life has been transformed. The gods have had a great battle.

There has been horrible carnage and destruction. It is time to leave our home. It is no longer safe here. Though the journey may be arduous, the gods will help bring us out of this land. They have promised us a good and broad land exempt from peril. This is their message, he said.

The journey from the only world they had ever known was long. Each step was alien Every sight, sound and smell was foreign. They scavenged for food, slept clustered under the stars and sacrificed nightly to their mute gods. Several clan members perished from fever, fall or famine along the way. Others quit from lack of faith. The gods want us to continue, the chosen one would say. They are with us. They will not let us fail. They will lead us to paradise. But no one else could hear the gods' exhortations. They put their trust in the chosen one. They had to believe. They had no other option. It was as if a special kind of hearing or knowledge, a divine gift, had been washed away by the rain and only their leader had been spared the dreadful deafness.

Finally, after many years, after passing through varied climes and challenges, the chosen one stood upon a small rise on a rainy afternoon and pointed to a bright green valley at the confluence of two rivers surrounded by thickly-treed mountains on three sides and a broad marshland holding back the sea on the other and said, Behold, the land promised by our gods. We have arrived. This shall be our home. Is it not beautiful? The gods have provided. The migrants looked at one another wordlessly. Then they wept.

They settled the valley. They built a long house. They erected a second structure, a church, where the chosen one and his descendants talked with the gods and the people could congregate to hear their holy words. They tilled the sweeping lawn of the valley. Farming displaced hunting. They netted fish in the rivers and built rafts to sail the sea. Their numbers grew. Children ran through the thick grass and learned to swim in the waters. This would be the only world the young would ever know. The elders still spoke of the old ways, but the younger members had little interest in the customs of the former, forsaken world. A new history was written and the old history became myth. A vision of hope replaced the fear of exodus. Time passed. No one marked the misty night when the last remaining elder who had heard the gods speak took her final breath. She passed away, as did all the others, without ever knowing why the gods suddenly went silent one rainy morning long ago.

The generations that followed knew not that gods once spoke to everyone. They received the messages of the gods through the priests, the holy ones, the direct descendants of the chosen one. Dispatches came only from the church. The gods told the priests when and what to plant and the priests told the farmers. The gods told the priests to domesticate animals and the priests told the people. The gods told the priests to spread their glory and the priests told the others. The gods told the priests how to run all their affairs and the priests told the village. The gods told the priests how to worship and the priests told the congregation. The priests told the people to spread the message far and wide. The priests told the people to multiply. The priests told the people how to live and how to die.

The long house was razed on orders from the priests. The inhabitants of the valley built individual houses, scattered throughout the broad plain. The valley and rivers and marshland and sea provided an abundance of food for the inhabitants. The tree-covered mountains burst with the materials necessary to build their houses and enlarge their churches. Strangers arrived from places unknown with foreign languages, customs and thoughts. The priests allowed them to remain once they pledged their fealty.

Word spread of the valley people's bounty. More and more foreigners arrived. The priests worried. The gods' told them they must protect what had been given them, so said the priests. Thus a militia was formed. The strongest and most able of the men made weapons and secured the valley. They built look-outs. They walled the center of the village. This new fear com-pelled the people to abandon their homes throughout the valley and move inside the protective wall. Strangers were no longer welcomed; rather they were questioned and harassed with great suspicion before being allowed inside. Sometimes those not allowed in formed disgruntled bands and attempted forcible entry only to be beaten back by the militia men. Over the years new, higher walls were built outside the old walls as the town grew. The descendants of the original militia assumed the important job of protecting the citizenry. This warrior caste grew alongside the priestly caste a step above the tradesmen, the farmers and the fishermen.

Self-preservation can rationalize many things. Hence protection comes in many guises. The warriors soon were not content merely settling disputes at the fortified village gates. They took to patrolling the outer reaches of the valley where people not of the village began to settle hoping to share in some of the bounty. The soldiers made forays into neighboring villages, conquering as they went. The warriors forced all to pledge their loyalty and thus greatly expanded the size and number under the protection of the village.

As the village's power and size expanded, control became an issue. The priests, the church leaders, needed two things: to spread their influence and to protect their status. They built more houses of worship and ordained more priests, but it wasn't enough. There were too many people with too many gods. Even their own warriors returned under the influence of strange beliefs, carrying unknown idols.

So the priests wrote a book.

In this book the priests catalogued everything they

could that would maintain their power and control over the rapidly expanding populace, and especially the warrior caste. The numerous gods were replaced by a single omnipotent being with whom only they could converse. Only the priests could decipher the word of this god. They set forth and categorized good and evil, right and wrong. They created eternal, horrific punishments for those who did not follow their guidelines. They created an afterlife. They created a hell. They codified fear.

Against all the known laws of mathematics, their one god quickly destroyed the hundreds of gods worshipped by most people. The Word of God, as the book was sold, proved to be more powerful than a thousand armies.

Once the rules for living had been written it was not long before more mundane matters were systematized. And government was born. The priests created entirely new (lower) echelons within their ranks to deal with the everyday governance of the people. Their power seemed as omnipotent as their God's.

The priestly plan was so successful an unprecedented prosperity befell the town. Guided by the new laws, both secular and religious, the townsfolk grew rich trading with others. Their proximity to the sea facilitated transit of goods and people. Exotic wares began to appear. The trading class became immensely wealthy, despite their tithing and gifts to the church. The town grew larger with enormous homes and broad thoroughfares. The town became a very big place. The town became a city.

The priests built more elaborate churches called cathedrals. The warriors were equipped with the latest weaponry. The governors passed laws. The port was dredged and fortified. And all this building, all this expansion, further lined the silk pockets of the businessmen savvy enough to access the power of prosperity.

There were still farmers and fishermen and coopers and cobblers. They hadn't gone anywhere. They just didn't matter much to the priests or the warriors or the governors or the rich. They were consigned largely to side streets and less desirable neighborhoods. The valley town slowly became segregated into rich and poor. Mansions and shotgun shacks shared the same street name, but had vastly different numbers.

Progress never sleeps was the new mantra. And nature must be tamed in the name of advancement. After all, God's book gave them dominion over the earth and everything on it. Marshland was drained to increase the size of the port. The rivers were diverted to protect the new downtown. The rainfall runoff from the mountains was controlled. A series of levees was constructed to hold back the sea. Sometimes these improvements led to greater flooding than normal but only in a few poorer parts of town. They called this progress.

Other engineering, scientific and cultural advances followed. They created artificial light so the city would never be dark. They installed a sewage system. They built automobiles that could outrace a horse. They talked through wires to one another over great distances. They invented a machine that could capture their voices. They made weapons that fired projectiles so fast they couldn't be seen. They killed from a distance. They mixed concoctions that when taken prevented disease. They measured the air pressure and purified the water. They wrote and read books on every conceivable subject. (Yet the most popular book was still the Word of God.) They made their buildings out of steel and glass. They grew more food using less land. They fished with machines, nets and large traps. They entertained one another with the arts of music, painting and performing. They invented the television. They went to the moon. They killed each other by the millions. They gave birth to the internet.

And through it all, the priests and the warriors and the governors and the businessmen still held the power.

A hundred generations removed from a dank rock-shelter a shining city in a once bright green valley had been built.

And they called this city New Johnstown.

HAVE YOU HAD ENOUGH logorrhea from this insignificant, superannuated animal yet? Have you? Do you even know what superannuated means, you ignorant punk? Don't worry, you will. Or maybe you won't. Stop staring into the darkness and pay attention. You might learn something.

What are you looking at? There's nothing to see, anyway. Are you listening or not? You know I don't have to continue. This isn't exactly pleasurable for me, you know. And in case you've forgotten, you asked. Remember? Hmmph. That's better. Now where was I?

-isms

The simple rule of thumb is to stay away from all -isms. They are rarely good for you. I won't provide an exhaustive list; there are far too many. Even you could probably come up with a few. Yes, that's right, Einstein, racism is one. Racism is bad. Misogynism. Also bad. Some -isms are so bad they even attack, like botulism. Yuck. But the really dangerous ones, the ones that can change the history of the world, are things like elitism and jingoism. These are examples of big, powerful ideas, big -isms, that can infect and inflame the weak-minded and morph into the death and destruction of millions. Ideas are always stronger than brute force. The take-away from this is that in general -isms are like clubs. And you don't want to join these clubs. No, not botulism, I was just making a point. These -isms are mostly dogmas, they're inflexible, and they will lead you astray. Anytime someone tells you he is a proponent of some -ism, run. These are the same type of tractable sheep who mindlessly goose-stepped through 1930s Germany; and, believe you me, they will be on to another -ism before you can say amorphism. Nothing, never mind, just a little joke to myself. Yes, you're right, there are some -isms that are good. Altruism, how's that? It doesn't get much better than that. And, yes, very good, I am being a little dogmatic telling you to stay away from all -isms. You may not be such a hopeless cause after all. Yes, right again, that *was* a flicker of optimism. Touché.

Transportation (Driving, Commuting)

We all need to be somewhere else. We all need to get someplace. And, of course, we're usually in a hurry. We don't want to be late. God forbid we are late.

Giving people the right to drive is akin to giving them deadly weapons. Now, some people are capable of handling weapons, others are not. Most are not. A middle-aged woman was recently—this is true, look it up—sentenced for killing another motorist after her car broad-sided his while she was doing her nails. This genius was polishing her fucking nails and trying to operate a motor vehicle at 40 miles an hour. I don't know if prison can rehabilitate the stupid.

Some of us understand how dumb other drivers are so we opt for public transportation. Now there are only two problems with public transportation: it's public and it's public.

The first public sucks because public transportation is forced to transport all of the public, provided they pay the fare. And let me tell you something, the public on public transportation is unlike most any other public. This isn't the opera crowd. These are the dregs, the ne'er-do-wells, the sorry afterbirth of humanity. In general they are truly disgusting. My question is, where the fuck are they going?

The second public is that public transportation is run for the public by the public, usually by some mismanaged municipality. Such management virtually ensures that their operators are undesirable, unbalanced, unreliable, uneducated, unpleasant, unfit, unaware, untrained, unreasonable, unmotivated, unsanitary, underhanded, unethical, unbearable, unhealthy, unstable, uncooperative, unattractive, unscrupulous, uncivil, uncaring and unintelligent. To be honest there isn't a whole lot of difference between the crap driving the bus and the sewage paying for the privilege.

Those are—or at least those were—your options

for transportation: death by many or death by one.

Education

Human beings are by nature curious. But this doesn't mean we understand what education means. You know I'm pro-education. I am. I think it's imperative for both society and individuals. But let's face it, it's not for everybody. Not everyone is cut out to be a scholar. The world needs pothole fillers too. Yet with a blurry-eyed wink we try to pretend we are all the same. Crap like No Child Left Behind is killing education. No Child Left Behind?!? Of course some will be left behind. That's life. Any program that assumes, in its title no less, that it will work for every child is doomed from the start. Call it Some Children Left Behind or even Fewer Children Left Behind. At least then you're being more realistic and ingenuous about your goals. The program name is only the tip of the iceberg, though, isn't it? The crux, the real meat of the matter, is what are you leaving behind in your attempt not to leave anybody behind? The myopic obsession with testing a couple of predetermined skills is, it seems to me, closer to ignorance than education on the learning spectrum. The word education comes from the Latin *educare* which means to lead or draw out of. Thus education is, or was, or should be, the process of leading or drawing students out of their regular way of thinking. Instead we have No Child Left Before Inculcation. N.B. The word inculcate comes from the Latin *incalcare* which means to trample. So, rather than leading our children into better ways of thinking, we've decided to trample them with standardized-test-soled shoes. That sounds about right.

I could carry on for ages about the educational system or the lack of one. And I don't even know why I let myself get pissed off about the pathetic No Child Left Behind program. Ultimately no one gives a shit if one old man thinks there should be more Greek and Latin taught or that we're in danger of losing whatever humanity we still cling to if we fail to properly teach history and philosophy or that in literature you have the key to unlock everything. That's because they are all stupid. Administrators are only interested in the MBA sheen of 'new' ideas, metrics or systems. Educators care only about shorter work days and fewer of them. Well, in an effort to reach across party lines, here's something 'new' to think about. For the first time in history, due largely to the internet and its ancillary appendages, all the data, all the information you could ever desire, can be yours at the press of a button. Do you understand what this means? Can you see the implications? No longer should students have to spend (waste) their time memorizing the minutiae that was requisite in our (now antiquated) educational system. The information is there instantly, for everyone, always. We should be developing new ways for them to interpret, contextualize and synthesize this flood of material. The goal of the 'new' educators should be assisting students in managing all this information—most of it not worth the bytes it's made of. Because, I'll tell you something, if you're not careful you'll wind up with a generation of mindless fucks who believe everything that pops up on their iPhone or PDA or whatever and who will only be able to communicate using text shorthand and stupid emoticons. Or is it already too late? U R 2 L8 ☹ Game over.

Seasons

Some people love having seasons. They embrace the seasons. Others flee from the seasons. They deem them undesirable. Seasons may seem insignificant, paltry, undeserving of such attention. But, jeepers, everything I'm saying is undeserving, isn't it? Still, here you are stuck with an old man set in his ways and I'm afraid you'll just have to deal with my eccentricities. And remember, you asked. Where was I? Seasons, yes, I think there is something more to them than snow birds and sun worshippers. Don't get all hung up on your own experience of seasons: the big four. Not everyone on this planet shares your experience. For some there's a rainy season and a dry season. In other places they mark the seasons by the appearance or maturity of certain plants or when animals are in heat or migrate. My point is that the equinox to solstice and solstice to equinox eternal recurrence is the least interesting part of the story. Not to get all Ecclesiastes about it, but there's a time for everything and everything in its time. Yeah, you can look at this like some kind of cosmological metaphor about patience, but I think you'll find, in your inherent smallness, more to gain by accepting that millions of years of evolution have shaped us to be in tune with our seasons. In other words, you can't fight Mother Nature.

Evil

This is a good one. If you've been paying even half attention to anything I've said you'll understand that I think there's a lot of bad shit out there. Furthermore, most of the bad shit is done to people by people. Even a pea brain like you would admit that this is beyond dispute. But, outside of cartoons, I think we get ourselves into a pickle when we label something as evil. Rarely do we use the word in an accurate, surgical way like, 'it was an evil deed.' No, we like to carpet bomb things with the word, like in the phrase, 'Axis of Evil.' Mwah, ha, ha! We use it to differentiate ourselves from the truly heinous among us. Now you may argue, assuming you have the ability, that this is simply semantics. Sure, but isn't everything; isn't all thought forged in the smithy of language?

You think I'm splitting hairs here? Sure, former human beings like Hitler, Stalin and Pol Pot were bad, bad men. But evil? Or more often, pure evil? I'd be willing to give you insane, wrong, paranoid, brutal, psychopathic and criminal. Labeling them as evil, however, raises (or lowers) their actions to an exclusive classification, which makes them members of a club none of us ever want to join. They are somehow different than us. They are evil. The problem with this is who grants them this membership. It's not like people voted. Surveys weren't handed out. No, those judged evil are judged by the people who defeated them. That's why to most of the world Bashir is a war criminal and George W. Bush is just incompetent. That's why the U.S. decimation of its indigenous people was a regrettable, but not evil, chapter in history, while Milosevic's is. It is the winner who makes the rules, who applies the labels. The historians then pass this judgment on to the populace and we all live happily ever after in the knowledge that such evil could never happen again. Such evil is always an aberration. Evil is a black swan. Evil couldn't possibly be dwelling in us all. Denominating evil is the victor's final prize.

Happiness

And they lived happily ever after. That's the problem. It's our fucking fairy tales. We begin our lives spoon-fed this bogus pablum. We don't even know anything yet. How can we do anything else but believe in it? For Christ's sake, we're just little kids!

So we all grow up believing that beyond one certain point, after a certain rocky road, just over that mountain of misery, lies the promised 'happily ever after.' The Promised Land: our eternal happiness. Because to be happy we all were taught that it comes 'after' something. What that something is we know not.

But we know we must suffer first, and then we can be happy. So we live our lives convinced that the latest cataclysm, the most recent setback, our freshest loss is the 'after' we've been waiting for and we can live happily—beginning tomorrow. This fraudulent expectation is one of the reasons why our lives are so goddamned abominable.

At some point—I'm sure it's different for us all—you realize that you've been had. That it's all been a con. Happiness doesn't work like that. No one lives happily ever after. Humans aren't built that way. Happiness, if you're lucky to see any, comes in tiny little moments, unexpected and brief. The older you get the more you call upon memory to help relive those packets of pleasure. More is better. And at the end you add up the quanta of happiness you remember and judge for yourself whether you had a good life or not, whether you were happy more than you were sad and whether any of it was worth the trouble.

Television

Although I don't believe this will be an issue in the future, the shear asininity of television screams for comment. In the coming years television as it was invented may cease to be or else be such a different animal that it might as well have died. Then again, maybe we just need another word for whatever television has or will become? I don't know. Anyway, for my purposes, consider 'television' any megahertz picture/sound transmission, okay pinhead. I don't give a damn if you are holding the picture in your hand or it's a 3-D hologram or whatever the hell you kids are into. It's still TV to me. It's still the same concept. Besides, my complaint is largely about the content, not the technology.

I'm sure the creators of this technology (who I assume are happily long dead) would be rolling in their graves if they could experience the somnifacient crap broadcast in the name of their invention. You know even the word itself, television, betrays their sympathies: *tele* (Greek for far) + *visio* (Latin for sight) = far sight. Let me ask you this, how fucking farsighted is *The Jerry Springer Show* or *Fear Factor*? It didn't have to be this way. The magic (yes, I said magic) that allowed us to witness man landing on the moon is now nothing but a sad barometer of how low the common denominator can actually get. Christ, even the newscasts have dispensed with the pretense and are nothing more than tendentious coat racks for advertisers. Airwaves are used to brainwash, cajole, mollify. TV is the friend who goes away with a click. TV is our babysitter. TV makes you feel good. TV is a 24/7 Quaalude. And, yet, despite the almost universal agreement that most of what we watch is pure shit, the common bipeds will kill themselves for the opportunity to be on it, to be miniaturized, to be ridiculed and used in the erroneous hope that their appearance will be a first-class ticket to fame and fortune. You want a piece of advice that's simple and pragmatic? If you want to be less of an idiot watch less TV.

Internet

It took a few years but the bloom is finally off the rose of this turd, don't you think? I mean when the internet burst onto the scene it was new and cool with infinite possibilities. And yet, like everything else with potential, we managed to dumb it down. It's become a tool for tools to tell other tools what miserable lives they are having. All this Facebook, MySpace, LinkedIn, Twitter twaddle appears to be the limits of our imagination. Fantastic, I now have the ability to instantly tell some retard half way around the world that I just ate a grilled cheese sandwich. What a fucking coup for humanity! One day, and I hope I live to see it, all these social-mediacs or whatever you call them who've spent half their lives updating personal pages and spreading their minutiae of mediocrity are going to be struck by a thunderbolt of realization that they were, perhaps, the dumbest, most short-sited generation in history. I can hear them talking to their children or grandchildren, 'Oh, yes, and we posted everything. We let the entire world know what we were up to, what we were thinking about and what was happening in our lives, the good and bad, everything. We posted it all and it stayed there . . . *forever.*' And their children, with the wisdom and sarcasm that only comes with youth, will reply, 'How could you be so fucking stupid?'

I shouldn't be entirely negative, however. Porn has never been easier to access.

Yeah, yeah, I know the internet has everything. That's the fucking problem. Anyone and everyone can post anything. Sure you can immediately find the answer to any question, but you can also find a million answers. There's no filter, there's no ranking, no order. It's information overload. It's like you stirred up everything humans have ever known and thought into a giant electronic stew and given everyone a big ass spoon. How do you think it's going to taste? Sure now and then you'll get lucky and some chunks might not make you vomit, but most gobbets are going to be bloody awful. It's a numbers game. Most of the time you'll be eating crap. You might argue that our palates can detect the difference. I'm afraid you're giving the grazers too much credit. The goddamned Chinese are quoting comedy news sites as authorities for fuck's sake.

I'm not saying the internet is all bad, just mostly. Use it, but don't rely on it. And don't let it use you.

News

I'm not too old to remember that there was a time when news meant something. Things happened. Significant things. The War Is Over. The Eagle Has Landed. The President Has Been Shot. And we read about it in a NEWSpaper or someone we respected told us about it over the radio or said it to our face through the TV. Today things happen too, of course, but so many things seem to be happening all at once we no longer know, or are no longer told, what it all means. We all used to worry about the same things. The country was in dire straits or it wasn't. We were at war or we weren't. People were killed, but not so fucking many, every single goddamned day. Or at least we didn't hear about it.

So what's news today? And, perhaps more importantly, who determines what's news? We are in two wars that aren't really wars. How long is this news? We're in a prolonged recession and the rich are getting richer. Is this news? Is it news when 800 lives are lost in a Bangladeshi ferry accident? Then why is this trumped by a video of a dog trapped in the ice in Wisconsin or by Mel Gibson's or Charlie Sheen's latest drunken tirade? Should we judge by the number of hits or views or comments? Do we throw everything that happens on the giant wall of information and see what sticks? Won't cuteness, happy endings or schadenfreude always outsell the sad, sober truth about life? Surely there's a better way. Surely there is still news.

Rent vs. Buy

Okay, here's something utilitarian. Here's pragmatism for you. Don't get all excited, I'm not really going to tell you what to do in every case. As always, my words are merely signposts, floating signifiers. Anyway, why rent when you can buy? Simply put: the concept of ownership is largely illusory. Yes, we all agree that when you buy something legally you are its owner. But who or what gave the seller the right to sell it in the first place? Did she in turn buy it from someone else? Did he make it out of something they bought? You see eventually someone at sometime could claim that you do not, in fact, possess ownership of said item. Indigenous Americans are still shaking their collective heads over us owning and selling land. The whole thing seems very parochial to me. Renting, on the other hand, shares the ephemerality of all living things. There's a nice logic to it, don't you think? Why pretend to be an owner of something that sure as shit will in one form or another belong to someone else someday? Such pretense inexorably leads to pleonexia anyway. So don't squirrel away all your money hoping one day to own some fabulous object. It isn't worth it. Enjoy today. Enjoy your life. Go out and spend those pennies on a delicious, decadent meal and a nice bottle of wine. After all, you're only renting.

Fashion

Between haute couture and survival lives fashion. Most of us, rightly and thankfully, do not think much about either fashion extreme. Like in everything else we tend to live in the muddled middle. So what does fashion mean to most of us? Well, sadly, it heretofore meant a hideously unappealing compromise between pseudo-comfort on the one hand and an oblique notion of style on the other. This unholy alliance gave us leg warmers and mullets, parachute pants and tube tops. Three words: paisley Nehru jackets. To be sure fashion changed, but it never seemed to change for the better. It used to be that men wore suits and women wore dresses. Yes they were threadbare and unimaginative, but at least there was a style to them. Today it seems half the population wears sweats wherever they go. Comfort has broken the treaty. The fashion détente has ended. And comfort is winning. Nothing good can come of this. I know this is probably just a by-product of our general obesity, but do we have to make things worse? Have we surrendered? Fashion helped us attract mates. It made us, however superficially, feel better about ourselves. No one will convince me that velour sweat pants and flip-flops make one more confident. It would be a shame to consign the ascots, spats and zoot suits to the fashion bin of history all in the name of comfort. I'd rather we return naked to the garden. A well placed fig leaf at least hinted at style, however minimal.

Health/Medicine

Here's my issue with doctors, medicine and health in general. Part of it stems from the fact that if I'm going to be killed I'd rather it be at the hands of someone with a gun and some passion as opposed to some dour doctor ostensibly trying to make me healthier. That's number one.

Number two is the whole conceptual framework behind most medical treatments. Now, I'm not talking about washing your hands or treating a fever with some aspirin. I'll do that. I'm not crazy, you know. Nor am I talking about setting a broken arm or amputating a gangrenous limb or saving someone from cholera or treating lung cancer. No, I'm talking about cholesterol levels, blood count, electrical conduction, lipids, serotonin levels and blood pressure. I'm talking about biostatistics, informatics, cohort studies and relative risk. That's what I'm talking about. At some juncture the medical community—whether called the AMA, the CDC or the WHO—was hijacked by the epidemiologists of the world. And since that time every doctor on the planet has practiced evidence-based medicine or, in other words, probabilities. Now the thing with probabilities is that they don't mean shit in individual cases. And from my perspective I am an individual case; the only individual case that matters as a matter of fact. So don't tell me that my cholesterol is too high and I need this drug or that my blood pressure is not in the heart of the bell curve so I need that medication. I don't want to hear it. Because for all they know my genetic make-up puts me outside the curve, outside their norm, and trying to force fit me into that norm could be doing untold damage to my body. In other words, their attempts to fit me into their understanding of probabilities could kill me. No thanks, doctor. I'll role the dice with my million-odd years of DNA if you don't mind. Treat the goddamned person, not some pie chart.

Besides, if you're going to die why make things worse? Why spend the final hours of life in a battle with some medication? Suck it up, say good-bye, and let the living move on.

Wealth

Money may not be able to buy you happiness, but wealth sure as hell can. Ah, you're not as dumb as I thought. Yes, you're right. There are all kinds of wealth, aren't there? This gets to the crux of what it means to be human. How do we score our lives? How do we rate ourselves relative to others? Monetary wealth is one way. But you can't take it with you, although you can boldly leave your name behind on the wings of hospitals or the halls of museums. How about those who possess a wealth of intellect? I know more than you so I'm happier. That doesn't sound right. I'm smarter so I lived a better life. Again, that doesn't really resonate. You may have a wealth of offspring. Apart from bequeathing your genetic code, does this make your life any better or worse than the childless philanthropist surrounded by friends and admirers? No. Here's the thing. And pay attention. Wealth is always in the eye of the beholder. If you think you're wealthy—in any arena or in all of them—you are. Just don't covet wealth because someone else values that wealth. That's the river to disaster. Only you can fill wealth with meaning. You have to figure it out for yourself. Let the poor saps envy you for being you. That's their fucking problem.

Family

Just because you are lucky or unlucky (select as appropriate) enough to share genetic code with another human being—you are considered family. And in return you are forced to go through all the trials and tribulations life throws at you with these strangers breathing down your neck. Far from being comforting, far from succor, it is like you have these oppressive shadows hovering over you every minute of every day, until at last you are old enough to legally break free. You then spend the rest of your life trying to build something outside their shadows, but it is futile. They won't let you go. It's Cosa Nostra. No one gets out alive. You can't escape. They will hound and haunt you until death. They will remind you of the time you wet your pants in the second grade. They will show your wife a grainy photo of your very tiny and very prepubescent penis. The labels they gave you at eight years of age will forever remain tattooed on your forehead. You aren't Senior Vice President of Development. You are Sir Farts-A-Lot. You know Sartre was right on with the whole 'hell is other people' thing. But family takes other people to an entirely different level. Oh yeah, you're saying, your mamma loves you and all. Yes, indeed. It's a love that cuts right through to the bone. It's a love that never heals. It's a love so seared into your retinas that it blinds you to the reality of life. Even the best families traumatize. That's their main function. And off we go charging into the great big world filled with all stripes of hopes and dreams doomed to spawn a family of our own.

Friends

At least they are better than family. That much I can say. You can choose your friends. Though sometimes it's awfully difficult to unchoose them. Thankfully friends come and go. There is, however, a period in your life, and for many that period never ends, when you define everything by your friends. During this period you can't be happy unless you are just like your friends, in every way imaginable. To be cool isn't some affectation. To be cool is to be you, which means a you accepted by others—your friends. Unless acknowledged by your friends, it doesn't exist. *You* don't exist except through your friends. Fortunately this outward looking adolescence ends for most of us. Later in life friends are used to help us up the corporate ladder and to provide alibis to our wives. We golf. We ogle women. We whine about being screwed by divorce attorneys. We talk about the 'glory days' when we defined ourselves by our friends . . . because youth is always glorious and full of promise. The irony of all this is that, although most of us grow out of the need for acceptance, it has come too late. Because the fact remains that our sclerotic, adult identities were first formed in the wet clay of teenage friendship. It's who we are, now and always. It's the memory of who we were. Thus, lamentably, we spend our middle-aged days trying to replicate these former friendships now on our own terms, or sadder still, fondly reminiscing about how they once were.

Music

Does anyone even compose music anymore? I mean real music, not the crap you kids call music. That's not music. That's noise, appropriated noise at that. I know they say that one sign of getting old is that you lose the ability to appreciate contemporary music. Well, then I've been old for a very, very, fucking long time. No. Forget what I said. It's not true. Let's start again. *Da capo*. Music speaks to us like nothing else. Who cares why or how it happens? For once let's not analyze the shit out of something, okay. For once let's just admit that as animals we respond to the various sounds we classify as music. And let's just leave it at that. Just because classical music speaks to me that doesn't preclude klezmer or industrial or technofunk or thrash metal or whatever from speaking to you. So I'm not going to default to my over-scrupulous nature and criticize your undoubtedly poor taste in music. Consider this a free pass. Consider music, musical types anyway, off limits. Feel free to enjoy it all, from a cappella to zydeco. You're welcome. Still, allow me to say a little about the quality of contemporary music. Don't worry,

I'm not going back on my word. I won't talk about the type, just the quality. There was a time when music was produced by genius. Beethoven, Bach, Mozart and Mahler were geniuses. Of that there can be no debate. Yes, genius is rare. But talent is not. Woody Guthrie, The Beatles and Bob Dylan were talented. The rest of popular music is merely competent. And I don't hear too much competence these days. Think about that the next time you're listening to your trip hop. *Smorzando*.

Stock Market vs. Gambling

They are the same fucking thing and don't let anyone tell you any differently. And they are both rigged in favor of the house. Wall Street wins, Main Street loses. Thus it shall always be. Don't let some analyst with a bunch of pretty charts tell you that he knows how to beat the market. A monkey can beat the market. It's called luck. Some monkeys are lucky, some are not. But no one can tell you which ones, at which time, will be the lucky ones and which ones will be the losers. The stock market is a service industry masquerading as modern day alchemy. Do not believe their lies. You want to play? Invest, don't trade. And invest conservatively over the long haul and you won't lose your shirt. Maybe. Pretty sexy advice, huh? If you really want to play against the odds just go to Las Vegas and gamble your money in an honest way. The pit bosses, croupiers and dealers steal your money with a smile, but at least they are honest about it. They practically tell you in advance. I know. Gambling is fun. It's a high. It's exhilarating. But make no mistake, you may win a few battles, but you'll never win the war. So go ahead—throw them bones.

Travel

Travel is a noun of differentiation. Traveling is a verb of primacy. We go places to see how different we are from others. We go places to see how much better we have it and, *eo ipso*, how much better we are than others. And then we come back to our dreary little homes and complain about the trip and wonder in amazement how people can live without high-powered showers and ubiquitous ice cubes. We take identical flat photos of the Great Wall and the Eiffel Tower and the Great Pyramids and Machu Picchu. But we fail to notice the woman crying on the steps of a church in Prague or the little boy urging his father's donkey down a narrow lane in Marrakech. Don't be one of these pricks! Yes, people are different. Yes, it may seem odd. That's the fucking point. Learn from it, don't condescend. Eat their disgusting looking food. Make them laugh at your mangled pronunciation of their language. Take the side streets. Buy a local a drink. Have fun. You're on holiday for fuck's sake. It isn't some test to pass, some check mark to make, some photo album to fill. It's supposed to be unpredictable. The wonder of travel is that it shows us that we don't have it all figured out, that there are a billion ways to live and to build and to eat and to love. You should come back from your trip energized in the knowledge that your life doesn't have to be exactly that of your neighbors. You should come back glowing from the awe that human beings are incredibly adaptable and amazing creatures. You should return a bit different. You should return a better person than when you left. That's what travel should be.

Alcohol

Never trust a man who doesn't drink and never trust a man who drinks too much. We are back to moderation, aren't we? Back to old Ben Franklin. Ben Franklin? Really!? Come on. He was one of our founding fathers for fuck's sake. Yeah, that's right, the dude with the key. Ah, you're playing with me, right? Good one. Yeah, yeah, you got me. Anyway, in his autobiography he wrote down a series of straightforward rules to follow in order to lead a happy and successful life and it was all about moderation. You've read it. Good. Good. Good for you. Now, what was I saying? Oh, yeah, alcohol. For me, alcohol is the one thing in this world that makes life a bit easier, a bit more enjoyable, almost worthwhile. Liquor blunts the shards of reality. *In vino veritas*. But real drinking is an art. To drink properly you must study and learn the necessary skills, because there's a fine line between the sweet, almost magical, effects of the elixir and the disaster of drunkenness. And this takes years of—often very enjoyable— practice. Beware drunkenness, however. A brief foray into the land of blotto may have permanent consequences: broken bones, prison or worse. I'm quite confident at least half of us have alcohol to thank for our existence.

IT'S YOUR DAUGHTER ON the phone, sir; she says it's urgent, his secretary interrupted over the intercom. Tell her I'm busy, I'll call her back in a bit. She says it's urgent, repeated the secretary. Oh for God's sake. Excuse me gentlemen. Cleveland Pike rose from his leather chair and ushered the two men into the reception area. Ms. Benson, please keep these men happy while I attend to this call. Excuse me, gentlemen, he said closing the large oak double-doors.

Yes dear, now what's so important? Slow down, slow down, I can't understand you. That's it take a breath. Now, try it again. What? Are you okay? Where are you now? But you're not hurt at all? He didn't touch you, did he? Just the bag. Do you want me to come down there? Okay. Whatever you want. Let me at least put in a call to the police commissioner. No, no, he's a friend and he owes me more than one. It'll be a friendly call. Yes, that's right. Everything will be all right. It's only a purse. These things happen. It could have happened to anyone. What can I do to make it better? Yes, I know it's traumatic. Don't worry about that.

Good. Yes, you sound calmer now. Yes, complete the paperwork. It was a crime, wasn't it? Okay. If there's anything else I can do, let me know. Okay. Bye sweetie.

He pushed a black button ending the call and swiveled his chair towards the ceiling-to-floor window in his office. He looked down from his perch to Claibourne Avenue, tiny figures scurried into the relative safety of office buildings, the slow moving Big River drifted black in the distance. This city has become a toilet, he thought, populated by animals and criminals. There was a time you could walk down these streets any hour of the day or night and never give a thought about your safety. Today you have to look over your shoulder with every step. It's a cesspool.

Cleveland Aaron Pike opened the door to his private bathroom and proceeded to empty his bladder. Well, the old pipes still work, he thought. As he washed his hands and looked into the well-lit mirror he saw every one of his eighty years etched in the face staring back at him. Studying the furrows he was well aware that he was not entirely blameless for the city's condition. Pike's Plumbing had made him wealthy and he had always been generous to politicians, the arts and a few select charities. But he also knew that he'd taken more out of New Johnstown than he'd put in. And isn't that the bottom line? The guilt of the aged, he thought, still staring in the mirror. We all could have done better, done more. Life isn't easy, though, you do what you can, what you have to. He tried to find reminders of his youth under the crepey skin, the angle of the nose there, a dimple in the chin here. An unrecognizable old man stared back at him unhappily.

Ms. Benson, please show my distinguished guests back in, if you would. Gentlemen, I apologize. I know your time is valuable, but this was a personal matter. Nothing fatal, mind you. My daughter, it appears, was the victim of a purse snatching this afternoon. She is uninjured, but as you can imagine shaken by the ordeal. You know how women are. Think nothing of it, I understand completely, one of the men said, I've got two daughters myself. My sympathies, replied Cleveland. Now where were we?

On the cement stoop of the shotgun house his mother rented, Robert 'Boo' Knight bit into a bruised apple. There was no school today for the high school sophomore. It was parent-teacher conference day, though Boo's mother would not be able to make it on account of work. Work was more important, thought Boo, it's not a big deal. Yet a part of him wanted his mother to hear his teachers' praises first-hand. Though everybody, especially his mother, knew Boo was smart.

His homework done for the week, Boo had decided to surprise his mother with dinner. He figured if he could catch a couple of decent-sized fish from the river, he'd be able to clean and cook them with some beans and rice before she returned from her cleaning shift at the hospital. He tossed the apple-core into the

57

gutter, sustenance for the rats—everybody's got to eat, he thought. He stepped back inside the house to get his plastic fishing rod and a book to while away the time, and then started toward the Little River.

Two rivers converged at New Johnstown before flowing into the sea: the Big River and the Little River. The Little River, the one nearest Boo's neighborhood wasn't much to look at. Years ago the city had removed the natural shoreline, replacing it with vertical steel and concrete embankments to keep it from flooding. This made it look more sewer than river. Nevertheless there were fish in there and in decent numbers. Mostly redfish and channel cats. And, of course, crawfish. Once in a while a lucky local landed a spectacled trout.

When he turned the corner and saw them stationed around Sid's Liquor and Groceries it was too late to change direction. He had already been spied. Hey Fuck Finn, where ya' goin? He ignored their taunts. Just keep walking. This is not about you. Their leader, a gigantic, mottled, drop-out, ex-con called C, approached him. Are you deaf? I said where ya' goin'? Just keep walking. The others surrounded him, not letting him pass. C grabbed the fishing pole and snapped it in two. Well, you ain't goin' fishing now, that's fer sure, he laughed, tossing the broken rod into the street. As Boo bent down to pick up the pieces one of them snatched the book from under his arm. Boo bristled and moved toward the thief. I wouldn't do that if I were you, hero, mocked C revealing a metallic handgun tucked into his waistband. Give me the goddamned book, said C. *Med-i-ta-tions* by Marcus something. What the fuck is this? It's not mine, said Boo calmly, it belongs to the library. Well, then, the library won't mind me borrowin' it from you, will they? Now get the fuck out of here before I get mad.

Boo did as he was told. He walked away. It isn't worth it, he said to himself. You'd have to kill each and every one of them. And there are countless others half-hidden in the shadows waiting to replace them. It would never end. He fingered the pieces of the fishing pole. I think I can fix it. And he headed down to the river.

Half a century ago Cleve began to dislike New Johnstown. Yes, it was his birthplace, where he founded his business, where he owned his home and where his daughter had been raised. But the city, even then, to Cleve's mind, had lost its way. One of the first things he did when he began to make real money was to purchase a lakeside cottage, a lakeside mansion really, at Three Mile Dam, a reasonable distance up valley from the city. The lake at Three Mile Dam had been expanded by the New Johnstown elite a century earlier in a still-born attempt to create a bucolic getaway for the well heeled. The dam itself, a mini-mountain of dirt, plant and rubble, looked anything but man-made. This was due to age and indifference—in equal parts. The barrier rose more than 70 feet in height and spanned more than 900 feet across. Its construction had swelled the once modest mountain lake to an estimated 20 million tons of water weight covering almost 500 acres. Some said this was the largest man-made lake in the country. Located up the valley some fifteen miles north of New Johnstown, the moneyed built this retreat, their private summer resort, to escape the noise and other irritants of the prosperous, industrial city. Cleve's 'cottage,' modest by the lake's tony standards, had eight bedrooms and nine bathrooms, a private dock for two speed boats and two sailboats and, of course, complimentary membership and access to the new 40,000 square foot clubhouse where he rubbed shoulders with the wealthy from New Johnstown and its environs. Although primarily a summer retreat, Cleve found himself spending more and more of the year tucked away in his mountain home. He particularly enjoyed the solitude of fishing. Early in the morning, a dense mist hanging over the fake lake, he'd unmoor his favorite boat and try his luck catching a few of the imported black bass the stocked lake was known for. That was where Cleve was happiest.

So what would happen if we just did nothing? Cleve asked the men. They think they've got us between a rock and a hard place and they're sitting back waiting for us to make a wrong move. Well, what if we don't move? What if we do nothing? Can we wait them out? Interesting, said one of the men. They certainly won't be expecting it. Brilliant, said the other. Let us run some numbers, talk with Legal and see how it shakes out tactically.

Dead on her feet, Boo's mother smelled the baking fish as soon as she opened the door. Boo, I'm home. Come on back, mama, throw down your worries. I've set the table. All you have to do is sit down, rest your weary limbs and let me serve you dinner. Oh, you thoughtful boy, you. Where'd you get all this? It smells positively scrumptious. You are too kind to your poor, old mother. Wearing a wide smile, Boo served his redfish mixed with beans and rice. They drank tap water with ice cubes from large plastic cups. Eat up, mama. How does it taste?

Thank you so much for everything, my boy. This was a lot of thoughtful, wonderful effort. I thank you. Aside from all this, what else did you manage to do today? Not much, you know, the usual. Reading and stuff like that. Nothing out of the usual, then? That's good. Well, I did have a run-in with C and them. Now, mama, I'm fine. They didn't even touch me, though they did a number on my fishing rod. Then how'd you manage dinner? Aw, it wasn't too difficult to rig something up. Well, I'm glad that's all that happened. Those boys are trouble with a capital T. They are indeed. Yeah, and they also stole a library book. Boo, if I've told you once I've told you a million times to keep those books inside the house. How much is it gonna cost us to replace? I don't know, mama, I'll talk to the librarian. Maybe she'll let me work it off or something. Boo, I know you didn't do anything wrong, but you gotta be more careful. Things cost money, you know. I know, mama. I know.

Following the PowerPoint presentation, Cleve pushed a tiny button on a tiny remote and the room gradually brightened. So, gentlemen, if I understand what you've just been saying, we will actually make more money by doing nothing. That's right, sir. That is the shared opinion of Legal and Finance. Given the contracted guaranteed minimums from the city we could technically, and we believe in actuality, move the materials and staging to our other operations out of state at no cost to us. In addition, the subsidiary would be able to claim a hardship which would greatly reduce the overall quarterly tax burden, both federal and state. This, however, is only our opening gambit. It gets even better, sir. Should they persist in their work stoppage beyond 90 days we would be able to invoke the *force majeure* clause, which would not only absolve us of any obligation, but the city would have to reimburse us for materials and labor, plus our commissions of course. Since we would have already repurposed the materials, this would be pure profit. It's a win-win. All for doing nothing. So what's my deadline to commit not to commit? We should probably begin moving within the next few days. Bottom-line, then, is that the city has to pay us for doing nothing. According to the contract, sir.

Yes. But only if we do nothing. None of this works if we utilize non-union workers in order to begin the project or if we even negotiate with the unions. We have to, in effect, maintain our innocence. Stay above the fray. We are the victims here. We contracted in good faith and had every intention of performing for the city. This is our story. And that's how we should frame this for the media, the city and its citizens. Very well. Thank you, gentlemen. This is all quite intriguing. I'll be in touch. Ms. Benson will show you out.

The library was Boo's second home, his sanctuary. Truth be told, he would have paid them to work there, had he any money. So when the librarian was informed of the missing Marcus Aurelius and conscripted Boo to a month of Saturdays and Sundays stacking, stamping and scanning books, his weekend plans were largely unaltered. Passing between the enormous Corinthian columns guarding the front door supporting the wrap-around garland façade dated in Latin was like entering a new world for Boo. Or rather it was like entering a thousand new worlds. Not only was this the warehouse of knowledge and success. This was the accumulated story-telling of a species: the imagination of all who have ever lived. And all of this was conserved with great care in disciplined order. There was a system and a rationale behind the system, a purpose for the way these worlds were arranged. To escape into the stories behind these columns was to escape with a purpose, an

63

intent, a goal. For Boo the library was both past and future. It was timeless.

On his very first visit to the library Boo told his mother he was going to read every book they had. His mother laughed and said something like, I believe you might just. Initially he thought he'd begin at the As and work his way through the alphabet and finish as a wise old man with the final Z. Of course at the time Boo didn't realize that 1) the books were not necessarily arranged in that manner and 2) books were constantly being added and subtracted resulting in a continuous undulation on the surface of this ocean of reading. Later, like most autodidacts, Boo realized the great gaps in his learning and was now at 16 working through the previously omitted classics: Plato, Aristotle, Homer, Aeschylus, Hesiod, Tacitus, Euripides, Boethius, Martial, Caesar, Horace, Aristophanes, Sophocles, Juvenal, Plutarch, Cicero, Pindar, Lucretius, Ovid, Vergil, Thucydides, Herodotus and, of course, the purloined Marcus Aurelius, all in translation. Late at night as he fell asleep he sometimes dreamt of fluency in Greek and Latin, but even the dreams of a smart, young man have their limits.

On occasion, whether he was working or not, Boo was asked to help a patron find a particular book. That first Saturday of his *Meditations* sentence a seven year-old girl, still shaking the raindrops off of her yellow plastic coat, politely asked Boo where the books on unicorns were. Unicorns, unicorns. Hmm. Certainly not here in the non-fiction area, he replied. Come with me. Come on mom, he's going to take us to the unicorns. Hey mister, what does non-fiction mean, she asked? Oh, non-fiction means prose writing other than fiction. That doesn't tell you much, does it? It means writing about real life, real things, not imaginary things like unicorns. But unicorns are real. I've seen them, the girl said. You have? Yes, I see them all the time on TV. They are my favorite animal. I see, answered Boo smiling at her mother. Well, here we are. Let's see. Ah, here's one called *Eunice the Unique Unicorn*. How's this? Perfect, she said hugging the book. See, she stated, pointing at the drawing of a unicorn on the cover, I told you they were real.

Cleve's daughter thundered into his office mid-sentence. I don't know why they call them civil servants; they weren't civil in the slightest. Oh, daddy, it was the most awful experience. I do not know how people survive in this city. How do they function? To be face to face with murder and death every single day, it's incomprehensible. That's what it is. *In-com-pre-hen-sible*. Oh, daddy. Tell me you'll get out of here. Move your office to the suburbs. This city is not fit for man or beast. Oh, daddy. Funny, he thought, it is either sir or daddy, nothing in between. Only Cleve to myself. There, there, honey. It was only a purse snatching. It could happen anywhere. And you're fine. And you got your bag back after all. It all worked out, didn't it? Well, for you maybe. But to have to go to that police station and answer all their questions and suffer such humiliations. It was almost unbearable. I made Geoffrey leave the club to come get me. I was shaking for hours. It was only your voice that helped me get through it all. Cleve felt it was his fault. Not for the purse snatching per se, not for the crime, but for her reaction to it. For the way she was. For what she had become. He had spoiled her. He had given her everything. She was his one and only angel. And this largesse had produced a spoiled and entitled young woman. Despite this realization, Cleve thought he'd probably do it all again, though deep down he had to admit that it was a happy day when he'd finally married her off, even to that repulsive rapscallion Geoffrey. Could you tell Ms. Benson to get me some water? I don't think I'll be able to describe the crime unless I've had my pills, she said. Cleve requested the water and began to daydream of crystal blue skies over his lake. He didn't want to hear the details, but he knew he had no choice in the matter. I had just left the bank (gulp), the one on Main. Geoffrey had phoned and needed extra for something or other and I was in the city for one of those silly board meetings. Well, I wasn't more than a half block from the bank when the unthinkable occurred. I recall struggling with my umbrella. It was very windy and out of the blue I was twisted and dragged to the ground. I think I may have struck him in the head with my umbrella. It flew God knows where.

It all happened so quickly. There was no warning whatsoever, just a push and a twist and there I was crumpled, like refuse, like a discarded wrapper, on the filthy wet pavement. I suppose I screamed. Somehow I managed to gather my wits about me and look up and I saw two black boys running away in opposite directions. The violence broke a heel off one of my pumps. After what felt like an eternity, a few people—tourists no doubt—helped me up, examined my contusions and scrapes and, finally, the police arrived and took me unceremoniously to their station. That's when I called you. I really don't want to relive the interrogation again. Suffice it to say that it was the most humiliating hour of my life. Oh daddy, I'm still scared. You simply must get out of this hell-hole—for me.

Boo left the library at the usual time which gave him ten minutes more or less to get to the bus stop. Thick black rain clouds abetted night's approach and the damp pavement reflected yellow city light. He skipped across Main Street, dodging shallow puddles, and took shelter under the concrete eave of the First National Bank. Looking out at the glistening city, trying to gauge the rainfall, Boo saw C walking down the street. There was something odd about his gait, like he was trying too hard to walk naturally. Then, like a shot, C exploded into a sprint. Boo instantly understood. A split second later C wrested the woman's purse from her shoulder without breaking stride. Boo, too, took off. He knew that C would turn the next corner and cut through the narrow alley between the theater and the parking garage. Boo could cut around and catch him just as he left the alley. As he ran, Boo didn't think about what he was doing or why he was doing it. His only thought was to beat C to the spot and get the woman's purse back. Had he thought it through he might have reconsidered. Panting as silently as he could, his heart pounding in his chest, Boo heard the slower footfalls of C approaching. He stayed low as he waited for C to round the corner of the building. He'd take him out low, let C's speed and mass do the work, like putting a stick in the spokes of a bicycle. Almost there. And, wham, Boo hurled himself at C's knees sending him dazed to the ground. Boo grabbed the purse but as he began to get up felt a tug on his ankle which tripped him face-first into the railing of a fire escape. Somehow he managed to kick the clawing hand away and dash into the twilight away from C's yowling threats.

Boo ran some twenty minutes, zigging and zagging through the city, unsure if C was even chasing him anymore. As he finally slowed, he examined his throbbing face where it had slammed against the fire escape. Mama will not miss this, he thought. Boo began to make his way home thinking more about what his mother would say than whether or not C knew who'd retaken the bag. The bag. What to do with it? He hadn't thought that part through. But, as fate would have it, he happened upon a local police station while walking home in the dwindling light. He looked around twice, then a third time, before climbing the stairs. Convinced that no one was watching, he tucked the bag into a corner where it was both safe and conspicuous. He descended the steps with the bounce of someone who'd just had a traffic ticket dismissed.

That sounds out of the ordinary, said Cleve. I assure you it is, answered the police chief. I've been doing this for 20 years and I could count on one hand the number of times we've recovered the purse and all its contents untouched. It simply doesn't happen very often. Well, I'm glad it happened in this case, said Cleve. So am I, returned the Chief. But to be honest there is little likelihood that we'll ever catch this guy. It's a dirty little secret that most of these small-timers have a pretty good return on their crimes. On the other hand he'll slip up sooner or later and he'll do his time for something else. That I can assure you. So you don't think you have enough to catch him, asked Cleve? Nah, we've got your daughter who was traumatized by the incident and then we've got one other witness who claims he saw the whole thing. But the guy is some tourist from Oklahoma only here for a few more days and I'm sure the story has grown ten-fold in his mind since the actual crime, the Chief laughed. One of my officers did catch a glimpse of one of them running, but states he didn't get a very good look. We'll try, but I don't want you to get your hopes up. Well, if there is anything I can do let me know, offered Cleve. I would personally fly this witness back into town if that's what it takes to get this animal off the streets. Understood, said the Chief, I'll call you with any updates. Thanks again, Chief.

Cleve gazed out of the window at the rising river. The rain is getting heavier, the drops are thickening, he thought. His telephone lit up. What is it? It's the Police Chief, answered Ms. Benson. Can't be, I just spoke to him. I know, he was laughing about it too. Okay, put him through. Yes. You won't believe this, said the Chief, but we got 'em. I think we got 'em. I don't have all the details, it just came across my desk, but it seems our perp returned to the scene of the crime. My officer recognizes the kid as he's walking out of the library, right around the corner from the crime scene. The goddamned library for Christ's sake.

Now don't worry, they can't see or hear you, stated the detective. They'll be out in a second and I just want you to take your time and tell me if any of them look familiar. But officer, I was so scared and he hit me from behind. Just do your best. Okay, send 'em in. You can do this. Remember they can't see or hear you. You are safe. Oh my, they all look so alike. They all look like criminals. Geoffrey, hold my hand. Take your time. Turn around. Let's see. Okay, face front. Yes. It is number three. Are you sure? I am sure of it. He's even got the mark where I struck him with my umbrella, which I've never recovered by the way. It's him. I am certain. Geoffrey, get me out of here. Now.

No. He's not up there, said the Oklahoman in a thick drawl. First of all he was way bigger than any of these guys. And he was piebald, can I say that? Piebald? Yeah, piebald, spotted. Like a horse. He had splotches all over. You sure? Sure I'm sure. Look I know this is my vacation, but if I could help solve a crime it would be worth a hundred vacations. But he isn't up there. Sorry, but I'm positive. I saw the whole thing. My wife was in shopping for some new shoes. I was outside the store and saw the whole thing. The guy was way bigger and splotchy. He's not up there. Sorry, wish I could've helped.

On the other side of the two-way glass Boo couldn't see or hear how his innocence was being debated. He shifted uncomfortably, afraid for perhaps the first time in his life. His mother, equally uncomfortable, sat in an adjoining room unable to process that Boo, her Boo, was suspected of being a criminal. As he turned around Boo replayed the interrogation in his mind. You were seen running from the scene of the crime. That's technically true, but I was going to get the purse back. By running in the opposite direction? Forget that. So you admit your involvement? I admit I got the purse back. How did I know how to get it back? How did you know to run in the opposite direction? How did you know where he'd be? Deduction? So you're a super hero and a fucking

Sherlock Holmes. You don't seem like you're an idiot, okay. You do understand how this sounds, right? Yes, I do. Boo took a deep breath. Listen, please. I did not steal the purse. I saw it happen. I took it from the guy who stole it. I left it at a police station. Wasn't everything still in it? Believe me, I'm the good guy here. Then tell me, who is the perpetrator, huh? Who's the bad guy? I know that you know him. Yeah, just what I thought. This is where you tell me something meaningless like he's big or has a tattoo or one arm. And why didn't you return it to the nearest station? Uh huh. Let me tell *you* something. Innocent people don't walk around for an hour holding stolen property. You probably even hit yourself in the face as part of your alibi. How would that provide an alibi, asked Boo, that would only further incriminate me wouldn't it? Don't be a smart ass, boy. You are in a lot of trouble. The woman you chose to rob, your victim, has a very powerful father. His friends are judges. This is his city and his system. I'd play ball if I were you. Save what little remains of your worthless life.

Gentlemen, we shall do nothing. They think they can force me between a rock and a hard place, well I didn't get where I am by playing by their rules. There's a win in every situation. Only losers compromise. Now, let's get this thing moving, but do it quietly. I don't want to tip our hand. Let's go over the media strategy again. We have to be very careful not to oversell our position.

Mama, you believe me, don't you? You know I didn't steal from that woman. You know I had nothing to do with it. Oh, Boo, I know it honey. But I'm flummoxed to understand how a boy so smart could do something so stupid. Mama, I am sorry. It wasn't something I planned. It just happened. It may not have been the smartest thing I've ever done, but I still think it was the right thing . . . given the circumstances.

Cleve's men left his office smiling. He took a few moments to congratulate himself on another business victory. Lawyers are sometimes worth their money, he thought. He never would've imagined as a young man struggling to build a life for himself that one day he would be making money, lots of money, by simply doing nothing, by providing no service, by using the system. But he has shareholders to keep happy and a daughter who doesn't understand the value of a dollar. This is business, he thought, just business. And business is business.

He looked off into the distance, through the cloudy skies, past the bend of the river out to the sea. He could still remember when the sea used to be miles away, now it practically lapped at New Johnstown's edges. Pike's Plumbing got rich helping the city grow toward the sea, eating up wetlands in the name of economic development. If it wasn't me it would have been somebody else, thought Cleve. For good or bad I helped, I tried, to make this city a better place. But his words no longer held any power. They had lost all meaning. He looked down at a city he no longer respected. He watched the small people run across the streets trying to avoid the fat raindrops that first fell past his grand office windows. It's a cesspool down there now, a toilet, he thought. My own daughter a victim of random assault. And they'll probably let the punk walk free. No, I tried to make this city better, but I'll be the first to admit I've failed. Why shouldn't I run my business profitably? This is why we draw up contracts for Christ's sake.

Cleve turned from the windows, sat down heavily in his big leather chair, started to reach for the telephone and thought better of it. He put his elbows on the desk and his hands over his wrinkled forehead, then rubbed his eyes and imagined himself alone on his boat landing the biggest black bass he'd ever seen. He imagined the solitude and the triumph. And, after reeling it in and removing the hook, he would speak a few secret words to the estimable fish before carefully and humanely letting it slip back into the cool, black water of the mountain lake.

The juvenile holding area was in the basement of the main police station. Boo was the only boy there and he wondered whether that was simply luck or they'd isolated him due to the particulars of his alleged crime. Above his head ran a series of narrow windows, not barred like they would've been on television, but covered with thick dirty glass that made it impossible to make out more than shadowy half-people and the tracings of spent raindrops. He sat down on the obscenity-etched metal bench.

Bookless, Boo thought about many things during his isolation. He thought about his mother's disappointment and the fact that she was losing work because of his actions. He thought briefly about being incarcerated. But he was innocent. It would never come to that, would it? He thought about C. Had C recognized him? Would word get out that he'd been accused of the crime? Was he safe in his own neighborhood now? Had he really ever been safe in his neighborhood? Had any of them? Wasn't his section of the city a stopping place, an interruption? Hadn't it always been? It was never meant as a terminus, a goal. It was a purgatory for the poor, a transit point between an early death or a slightly better life. Despite his learning, despite his classroom success, despite his grand plans and despite his intelligence, his future had always been uncertain. Was it any more uncertain now?

Yes. Thanks. I will have a bite. I could use a little drink too, what with all this blabbering. But just a bit. We should conserve after all. Or maybe you want to keep me chewing so I'll stop talking. Well, no chance of that I'm afraid. I'm just getting warmed up. Let this be a lesson to you the next time you ask such questions . . . should there be a next time.

Hobbies

What a stupid word fucking word. Hobby. It reeks of musty stamps, murdered butterflies and model glue. What do you do for a hobby? Today that asinine question is more often answered in the extreme. Oh, I skydive. It's such a rush. Or, I'm addicted to heli-skiing. I honestly don't know which is more idiotic, coin collecting or amateur spelunking. The whole idea of doing what you love as an occasional, part-time, activity strikes me as disingenuous at best. The hobbyist is either trying to prove something or trying to hide from something. I bet if you scratch the surface of most 'hobbyists' you would find they are driven by insecurity, fear, habit or desperation. But maybe that describes us all. If we're still going to have this conversation, let's all agree that we should at least change the word. And, by the way, if you are ever in the company of someone who answers the question with 'my hobby is my children' my advice is to club the person to death and put them out of their misery.

Pets

I'm always amazed by this. Why on earth don't these people just have children instead? Perhaps it's because if something happens to the pet they won't be thrown in jail. Maybe they just want to pretend to love something that's disposable?

Believe it or not, owning a pet is even more pathetic than being a hobbyist. At least philatelists don't pretend the stamps love them back. Are people so lonely, so desperate, so starved for affection that they feel compelled to imprison, name and 'love' small animals? And what's sad is that it's done in a perverse attempt to bring a scrap of ephemeral, fake happiness into their lives. They'd be better served purchasing love dolls. If you're going to pretend, pretend big.

Have you seen these people? Have you seen what they do to and for these barely functioning creatures? My God, they dress them up in sweaters and shoes and send them to places like the Barking Lot for nail trimming and hair styling. They have them written into their wills. They give them Christmas presents . . .

77

wrapped. They spend thousands of dollars a year on premium food because someone has convinced them that their 'babies' couldn't possibly be happy eating ordinary pet food. And then, my absolute favorite fucking part, the best part of pet ownership, picking up the shit. It's priceless. Men and women, young and old, rich and poor, all around the globe stooping and scraping warm feces from grass and asphalt, fishing for crumbed clumps in litter boxes, removing birdshit hardened newspaper from cage bottoms. What a treat to own a pet! What joy! Not to mention those dog owners unfortunate enough to dwell in cold climes. Oh, to don four layers of clothing at six a.m. in mid-winter, to step outside into a dark wind chill of -20 just so YOUR fucking PET can piss and take a dump. What bliss! What joy! And don't forget to pick up the steaming turd!

Oh, here's another tidbit for all you miserable, love-all-living-things, petaholics out there. A recent study has concluded that a dog's carbon paw print is more than twice that of an SUV. Pet that!

Art

Ah, painting, sculpture, music, poetry, literature. The human grasp for immortality. What is it about art? Almost every one of us has tried to answer this question. Well, those of us with half a brain that is. Offense intended. Frankly, if you knew the answer you wouldn't bother asking the question. I know that sounds mysterious. But art is mysterious or at least it should be.

What makes a human being want to create a work of art? Is it emotion? Is it faulty wiring in the brain? Is it for love or money, for fame or revenge? Why can some chosen people arrange colors or words on a page in such a way that it speaks to the souls of the rest of us? Why are Mona Lisa and Don Quixote enduring?

No matter. Art is us at our best. It is the human spirit briefly flying free of the gravity of existence. It is a hopeless attempt to break the unbreakable bonds of temporality. And therein lies its power, its honesty. Despite all the skill, despite the passion, despite its resonance, it is doomed to fail. For we are doomed to fail.

Sorry, was that too sensitive for you, you philistine? Too bad. This is not to say that all art is the same or that all art speaks to all of us in the same way. Hell, most contemporary art, conceptual art, installation art or whatever you call it strikes me as a con, a big joke on those who fawn, buy or gawk. I don't get it. But to tell you the truth I can't say why I love Rothko yet think Barnett Newman is crap or why Warhol speaks to me and Lichtenstein does not. That's art for you.

History

The thing about history is that we only have the events, episodes, stories, etc. that were recorded. But we all know that for everything that has been written down,

79

inscribed, depicted, or passed down orally, there are a billion experiences that have been lost forever. That being said, too many of us refuse to learn about our history, like it's some illness to be avoided. I'll side with Goethe here that 'he who cannot draw on three thousand years is living from hand to mouth.' If you do not study what has transpired throughout history you are unable to draw from it. Now this is not to say that history merely repeats itself; rather wouldn't you want to have all the information available before you make a decision, before you pronounce? It seems straight forward and simple to me. Yet here we are, living in our own age, once again convinced that this time things are different, that this time it's special. Had we learned our history we would know that no time is special, no time is unique. Had we learned our history we would see that we make the same mistakes over and over again. The rulers throughout history (and there are always rulers) have failed to grasp the unlearned lessons of their predecessors: provide the mass of people with a comfortable environment, sustenance, peace, and a light but equitable rein and all will be well. But fail to feed them, churn up their emotions, play upon their fears, juice them with jingoism or pit them against one another and it is only a matter of time before the rulers become the ruled. History teaches us that human beings are social animals in the best and worst sense of the word. History is there to teach us, but are we here to learn?

Sleep

Are you still listening, you little pissant?

There are few truly pleasurable things in life. Great food and drink and great sex make everyone's list. The best of them all, however, is usually and undeservedly omitted. Ah sleep, the peaceful playground of the imagination. Sleep just has to be good to feel great.

Why sleep has gotten such a bum rap I cannot fathom. The moron-majority typically speaks of it in the pejorative. 'You know we waste a third of our lives sleeping' or 'he's sleeping his life away.' Sure you can sleep too much and that might not be so good, but is eating too much (great or not) or having too much sex (great or not) any less dangerous. No, in fact quite the opposite is true.

Think about it. How goddamned important does sleep have to be when you consider that our forebears were literally risking their *Homo erectus* asses just to grab a few winks? Doesn't that tell you something about its value? And do I even have to mention dreams? For fuck's sake some of my favorite moments on this planet took place while I was dreaming. Hell, I can still vividly remember a dream I had 50 years ago about a woman with hair parted in the middle, blonde on one side, brunette on the other. She approached me as I sat at a bar and claimed she was an MBA specializing in ectopic pregnancies. Of course it doesn't make any sense. But she was hot and she was digging me and I still recall the feeling to this day. So don't let some smart ass tell you that your sleep consciousness is any different from wakefulness. Who the hell cares?! Life is life and whether you imagine the girl in the next cubicle digs you or that you can fly doesn't make a bit of god-damned difference. Enjoy your dreams, revel in them, and remember them. They are as real as any bullshit interior monologue you may create commuting to work. Bah, you poor bastards aren't even smart enough to grab the few crumbs of happiness that evolution has dropped right in front of you.

Maybe in the end the reason sleep is seen as an ugly step-child is due to its significance in memory processing. Maybe we are all too pissed off that sleep helps us remember what shitty lives we're leading. Maybe that's it.

The Telephone

The name itself turns you off, doesn't it? Well, for once and probably for the only time, I happen to agree with you. I can't remember the last time I heard someone say, 'telephone'. They're hardly telephones anymore are they? They do everything but make a goddamned call. Yeah, you're smiling, you little twerp. That's right, the only people who actually use the telephone to talk are old farts like me, right? Yeah, you geniuses tweet, text and Facebook. Brilliant. Okay, so the telephone isn't a telephone anymore. What is it? I'll tell you what it is. It's an albatross, that's what it is, a cheerily self-imposed millstone. Believe it or not the telephone once worked for us. It was a tool we used to communicate important things to others. It had wires and cords. It rang. It would hurt your ear if you talked too long. It was occasional. Today no one can leave home without it. It goes to the bathroom with us. We've practically sutured the damn thing to our hands, thumbs flapping at the ready. We ping our thoughts and location to the entire world without a care, without a thought. But what you don't realize is that the telephone no longer works for us—we work for it. It tells us what to do and who we are. It tells us what and who to like. It beeps and sings and buzzes and flashes. We are powerless. We are never alone. We are one with the network. We are sad when it is silent. God forbid the battery ever runs down. In iPhone we trust. *Diomedea exulans*, you dumb asses.

Morality/Ethics

People are always fucking this one up. Make certain you don't. There is a distinction between morals and ethics. Morality is how we ought to treat others. Ethics is how we ought to live ourselves. There's a distinction here, get it? Now I'm not going to tell you how you ought to treat others or how you ought to live. That's your business. Throughout history people have struggled with this and, should you even consider it for more than a minute or two, I suspect you'll struggle as well. I know I have. So, if you become a self-interested Hobbesian on the one hand or a utilitarian Humean on the other, remember that no one really gives a fuck.

Personally, I've rejected both. Ultimately what matters to other people is how they've been treated by you. And what should matter most to you is how you sleep at night. Don't fall for absolutes or easy answers. Life is gray. Do the best you can. And always remember that you'll make mistakes. And that you'll screw up sometimes. We all do.

Clubs

I know what you're thinking, you pubescent sex-fiend. You're imagining blinking lights, loud music and a dance floor packed with gyrating girls shaking their assets, aren't you? Well, sorry to disappoint, but that's not the kind of club I'm going to talk about.

Clubs, real clubs, are just hobbies without the glue. I just don't get the whole shared interest bullshit. I mean we share everything. We're human beings. We share the same food, the same air, the same diseases. Why, oh why, do we feel the need to form clubs and partake in some arcane, twisted, faux love for Corvettes or dogs or Elks or whatever? Do we need the ritual, the sense of belonging? We already belong to the same club—humanity. Why make it more than it has to be? Do people who belong to a model railroading club feel superior to those in the autograph club? Who's the bigger loser, the guy in the science fiction club or the one in the ham radio club? Okay, fine you share an interest in something. Fine. Talk about it, raise money, whatever, but why do you have to form a goddamned club? Why the secret society crap? It doesn't make you any different, don't you see that? It won't make you special. Then you've got your country clubs, right. And here at least they're upfront about it. They're about exclusivity. Their intent is to keep people out. Now that's the only type of club I'd have any interest in joining.

Yeah, I know, I can tell by your smile that your mind is picturing gentlemen's clubs, isn't it? Well, you're no gentleman so get the thought of artificially inflated hooters out of your mind. Sicko.

Democracy

Speaking of clubs. Sure it's all the rage. But you can't tell me that this is the last word in political systems. I just don't buy it. It's already fraying at its edges. Look, I'm a big fan. I don't see anything better on offer. It worked well for a while in the city-states of ancient Greece. It can work. But maybe it doesn't work forever. Maybe it has a shelf life. Maybe it can't get too big or encompass too many people. I don't know. When you draw it up on the whiteboard it looks nice, doesn't it? Democracy = the people rule. Yeah, that's a great concept, a wonderfully enlightened idea. We have finally arrived. But in practice it's been a little different, hasn't it? It's not the people who rule, it's their representatives. Uh oh. A crack in the dam. Now these representatives represent whom? Everybody? Those most like themselves? Those who speak out the loudest? Those with the most money? Those with high placed friends? They can't listen to everybody. They can't equally represent everybody. We all have varying interests, right? So what do they do? Do they represent their conscience? Do they represent the majority? Do they pick and choose depending on the issue? Do they vote based on long term or short term interests? Or, God forbid, do they vote in order to get re-elected? I don't have any answers. These are tricky questions. After all, the representatives are just people. At least they were until they were sworn in. Do they then become something else? Are they then superior? Have they then joined an elite club? My take on the whole thing is that anytime you have people trying to please some people it will inevitably displease other people. I know, sounds too like Lincoln. Maybe that's the best we can do. Maybe that's all we deserve. I just don't think we've heard the last word on governing. Ideas are too often shaped by events.

Free Will

Pretend it's real. Understand that it's illusory. Yes, it's confusing and, yes, it's contradictory and, yes, even nonsensical. This shouldn't be news. Boswell wrote that Johnson reported, 'All theory is against the freedom of the will; all experience is for it.' But it wasn't all that long ago that we thought the earth was flat. Don't be seduced by appearances.

Think of free will like you would a feeling, an

emotion. It exists, you feel it, but it is caused by some-thing external to you. It's a way your being interprets the world, a way it makes sense of the environment, its pleasures and dangers, all so you won't blow your brains out with a shotgun.

Consider this. Think about all the things you do in a normal day. There must be thousands, maybe even tens of thousands of actions in a single day. Now, how many of these acts would you say are intentional? How many are you willing? Are you intentionally moving each leg as you walk down the street? Did you notice that you scratched your left ear or that you took a sip of soda before biting into your sandwich? The point is that we do many, many things (too many) without being conscious of them. And if we are not conscious of them, how can we claim that they are intentional? And, if you are willing to allow that some of our seemingly 'voluntary' acts are unintentional, you should be able to consider the possibility that all of our acts are performed without the need for free will.

You might think this leaves us with a dismal, deterministic existence. But how much of life is about appearance? How much of everything we experience is about perception? This shouldn't devalue our existence in the slightest. After all, in the end, maybe it's the illusion that makes us human.

Time

I'm not going to sit here and rehash crap like 'there's

never enough' and 'it heals all wounds' and 'it flies'. Do me a favor and do not believe in time. Yes, I do seem to be telling you not to believe in some pretty major concepts. Thank you for noticing. At least I can see you are paying attention. And don't think I'm some kind of quack. Nothing I'm telling you hasn't been said or thought before. Parmenides, of course you've never heard of him. You have? There might be hope for you yet. Then you know that he contemplated this in the early fifth century BCE. He went even further and maintained that there isn't any motion either.

I won't bore you with the physics behind my thoughts on time. I won't go into the Many Worlds theory, explanations of the Wheeler-DeWitt equation or the collapse of wave functions. You certainly wouldn't be able to do the math. Let me simply say that, like free will, time serves a quotidian purpose in our workaday lives. But from a philosophical and scientific per-spective neither has much of a foundation on which to stand. Time is measured by change. There is no past, no future, only instants of time. Don't think that I'm alone here. British physicist Julian Barbour contends that what we experience as time is just a series of individual *nows* in a configuration space he calls Platonia, the result of mathematical properties attributable to matter. Okay, I see the blank look on your stupid face. I've gone overboard. I forgot my audience. My apologies, squire. In a nutshell, use time. It can be useful. Just don't go around pretending the damn thing is real, that it has properties, that it's magical. Time is like everything else we humans have created—half-assed if not outright wrong.

Love

There are all kinds of love, aren't there? Does this mean that love is a thing that can be applied to a number of objects or are there different kinds of love for different objects and we are without the vocabulary to distinguish between them?

My vote is for the latter. First of all I don't think we are very scrupulous in our use of the word love. We love our homes, our pets, our family, our friends, our cars, ice cream, a bottle of Château Pétrus, 'that show'—whatever the latest hot TV show might be called—'that song', 'that book', *ad infinitum*. So forgive me if I think we kind of throw around the word willy-nilly. Here's what I think—I think that love should be reserved for your feelings about people. Period. Full stop. There should be no loving of animals or food, only people. And there should also be restrictions on the type of people you can love. For instance, you can only love those people who are family, close friends, those with whom you've had sex or those with whom you've been in battle (and I mean real battle, actual warfare, not some imaginary skirmish over PTA funds or something). Furthermore, since I'm making the rules, if people wish to use love in any other sense I should have the right to kill them on the spot. I would be doing a service for humanity. If we continue to dilute the meaning of love, it will lose its unique power. Either that or we'll end up with some hippy, Zen world of long-haired nudists, chanting bad poetry. I find neither scenario particularly palatable.

Sexes

Why, when our experience and our senses tell us otherwise do we persist in pretending we are unique among the animals on this planet? In almost every species you can see a clear distinction between male and the female. That doesn't mean that one is better than the other. It's just that they are different. Life, for whatever it is worth, is built on variety. Can we just accept that this is true for *Homo sapiens* as well and move on? Who gives a fuck if our brains are wired differently or that men grow facial hair but go bald or women bleed from the inside each month. Let's just admit that one of the inherent charms of animal life is that sexes are distinct and be done with it. Once we accept this we can embrace the objective fact that males and females do things differently, that they have varying strengths and weaknesses. And doesn't this expand our potential as a species? I mean wouldn't we rather build on the differences and utilize our strengths instead of dragging everyone down to some common, negotiated 'level playing field'? Now, don't get all bent out of shape and think that I'm advocating separate rights for the sexes. Although I'd like to get my hands on who thought that unisex bathrooms were a good idea. I'm not. I just think we'd be better served by accepting the differences between us rather than pretending they are chimeras hatched by unenlightened minds. *Vive la différence!*

Sex

For pleasure only. Please do not use for procreation. The preceding caveats should be plastered on every middle school wall in the world if we had any sense at all. In fact, if I had my way the only time people would have sex is with hookers. Prostitutes: gluttons for penisment. Get it? Sex with loved ones just screws up—pun intended—the relationship. Sure sex feels good. Can you imagine doing it without the pleasure payout? Now, you're just a kid. You haven't had enough time to do really stupid things in the name of sex. Try and imagine you're an old man like me. Picture putting yourself through all those years of work and humiliation without it feeling good. It would be unthinkable. Luckily, or not, it feels good. But, like everything else, we have to take something simple and pleasurable and mess it up. Today it's got to be about power or sadism. We tie ourselves up, employ animals, piss and shit on each other. Christ, the *Kama Sutra* is a kid's cartoon compared to what we do to one another. We can't leave well enough alone, can we? Pleasure's not fucking good enough for us. So let me see if I've got this straight. Nature gives us this really gratifying, enjoyable experience so that we'll do it more often and produce more human beings. So far so good. We do this for a few million or a few hundred thousand years, whatever your calculation may be, creating new positions, finding new ways to plant the seed. Okay, that makes sense; we are always trying to improve upon things—that's in our nature as well. But, then, at some point, post-consciousness, we decide that this act of pleasure actually means something other than the act of procreation. We de-link it from evolution. We change its purpose. It becomes a way to overcome your insecurities, a way to rebel. Some of us throttle our partners to within an inch of their lives in the pursuit of heightened orgasm. Really?! Hey, fellas, one thing is for sure—there's always another orgasm. Here we are, then, at the end of things and we've completely turned the whole sex thing inside out. An act that began as a way for us to further our species is now performed almost exclusively to achieve some imaginary perfect orgasm. Well, good luck with that. Every orgasm is good. My advice is to value quantity over quality. And wear a goddamned condom. All we need is for the likes of you to breed.

Aging

The only remotely good thing about getter older is that I expect it means that I have less living to do.

I don't want to get all poetic because you wouldn't appreciate it anyway. Oh, what the hell. Isn't all this more about me anyway? Aging is like train travel: you may rock to the unremitting pulse of motion and smile as life's features and faces flit past your window at varying speeds, but only upon alighting once a decade or so do you realize that you are not *where* you used to be and you are not *who* you used to be. Everything is familiarly foreign. The mirror of the moment reveals itself. You have aged, irrevocably. And even before your insight loses its incipience, the whistle sounds to call you back on board . . . and despite all entreaties the train keeps a rollin'.

Ah, that's a load of horseshit, right? It doesn't matter. Getting older sucks . . . even if you are one of the 'lucky' ones without a major illness or two—by the way they call that healthy aging or optimal aging, if you can believe such oxymoronic claptrap. Golden years, my ass. Do you want to know what age does to you? Gravity tugs on every inch of your body in an unrelenting effort to turn you into a two-legged Shar Pei. Your joints ache. People call you sir or old-timer and girls no longer notice you. You get all wrinkly and start smelling—putrefaction not olfaction. Everything moves faster than it used to. Hair vanishes from your head only to appear in the most singular places. You can't remember things, not that you want to anyway. The light is always bad and everyone whispers. A bruise may last for months. You don't sleep well so you wake up at 4:30 a.m., but by the end of the day you're so goddamned tired you go to bed at 7:30 p.m. Food

93

doesn't taste like it used to and chewing becomes a chore. You stop looking in mirrors. People die on you . . . one after another. You are irrelevant.

Don't be fooled by those idiots—most of them young—who claim to venerate this cellular senescence or whatever you want to call it. There are no leaps of knowledge, no hard won wisdom, no sense of serenity. Such are simply symptoms of an attenuating brain . . . nothing more.

I will tell you one thing, though. Don't wait to live. No age is guaranteed. Don't put things off. We've lost our urgency. In times past, life was short and dangerous, so people lived with a purpose, an urgency. Today, we all believe that we'll live to be 100, so we defer life, put things off, procrastinate. We no longer live our lives; we exist. Don't be tricked by this false expectation of longevity. Earn your old age, don't plan for it.

Government

I know I mentioned democracy earlier and I suspect your pea-brain doesn't understand the difference, but pay attention. Democracy is one possible form of government. There are many others. What I want to raise here, however, is why? Why do we need government at all? I understand that we're social animals and all. I also understand that for some reason we value freedom quite highly. It's this tension that makes it so difficult to develop a government that can last for more than a thousand years or so. Yes, I suppose we must live in communities for protection, socialization and so on. Though as technology progresses the term community will change significantly I suspect. No matter what our communities look like we'll always need rules and administration, right? Certainly we have to have rules. We couldn't function, whatever that means, without rules. After all, we all appreciate that we are animals susceptible to unpredictable, bestial urges. And we must select some of these animals—ideally the less unpredictable and less bestial among us—to create, administer and adjudicate the rules. Furthermore—these rules and administrators—this government, has to protect us, right? We can't let some other community just come and take what we've worked so hard to attain. This government should take care of us too. What good is a community of half-starved, angry, disease-ridden, homeless, uneducated, riotous, unemployed beasts? Who would want that as their community? But here's the catch. They can't take care of us too well because for some unknown reason that would endanger our undefined, nebulous concept of freedom. The more rules you make—however well-intentioned—the more rights you lose and freedom is impinged. So goes the argument. And, although freedom has a million different meanings among a million different animals, it must be protected at all costs, even if it includes the loss of the community itself. It all seems rather circular, this government thing.

In the enlightened end, maybe, we'll all be able to select the type of government we want based on our personal freedom quotient. Those who want more freedom but less protection can opt for one form of government, while those who value freedom above all else may select another. And perhaps we could migrate from one to the other like the migratory animals we are. People could, then, vote with their lives what form of government suits them at any given time. And we could all ebb and flow like the sea.

Dirt

I hate dirt. I hate being dirty. It's terribly uncivilized. I'm a clean man. I know. This is killing me. Yes, you can wash it off. You can clean up. This I also know. I think perhaps it's that dirt is a foul reminder that the world is inhabited by millions of disgusting creatures. After all, most dirt contains microscopic animals blindly wriggling and writhing, feeding on trash or one another, doesn't it? Deep down I'm afraid—maybe we all are— of things that are too small. And too big for that matter. These unseen entities are everywhere, in our food, on our skin, swimming in our mouths. It's goddamned disgusting. I have no desire to be reminded that we are merely bit players in the food chain. Dust, you know what dust is? It's mostly dead human skin. If that doesn't give you the shivers nothing will. So forgive me if I find this a little stressful. Forgive me if I'd rather be clean.

Terrorism

Yeah, I know this should be in the -isms category, but it's so terrifyingly pervasive and so goddamned misunderstood that, trust me, I'm doing you a favor by setting it apart. Now, whether you want to believe it or not there was a time when everyone in the entire country—hell, the entire planet—thought their life was going to end in a nuclear holocaust. We responsibly drilled an admixture of fear and false hope into a generation of little children by making them practice hiding under their school desks. Brilliant, wasn't it? Every new test and each new bomb design was front page news. We were told we lived under a new sun. And this new sun was going to destroy us all. It was just a matter of time, a brief matter of time.

Well, we didn't all die, did we? Sure you'll still find some fucked up fear-mongers who to this day say that we were close to the end. But that's all bullshit. No, we didn't all die. There was no blinding ball of light, no nuclear winter, no doomsday. What we did was exert an awful lot of effort and generate a ton of angst living through it. The over-heated imaginations and egos of a few folks in the Pentagon and the Kremlin held the planet hostage for decades and we all obediently swallowed their trickle-down fear.

What am I talking about? It's an analogy, you stupid prick! For fuck's sake! You really are hopeless, aren't you?

Terrorism is *your* generation's Armageddon.

Apparently every generation is prescribed one. Only it's all made up. It's all fiction. It's just a way for those in power to hold onto their power. So, instead of training you to distrust anyone who speaks Russian, they now train you to distrust those who speak Arabic. Instead of looking to the sky for missiles you look to your neighbor's skin color. Every unattended package is a bomb and everyone acting suspiciously is out to destroy your way of life. Wyoming gets federal funds to fight 'terrorism.' Wyoming. Enough said.

Here's a piece of advice. Focus more on who is defining 'terrorism' and who profits from you being afraid than trying to psychoanalyze or socio-analyze the so-called 'terrorists'. Maybe your life will be a little happier. Maybe.

THEY HAD WARNING: NO thinking person could say that they weren't warned; the truth of the matter was that they had warned themselves for years: they knew evacuation orders had been issued, they heard the stentorian declarations from politicians that prudence necessitated precaution, but the human thought process is a complicated amalgam of emotion, pattern recognition, history, habituation and just plain foolishness: 849 millibars, 25.07 inches of mercury: the sixth extinction: the storm meant nothing to you, you thought you were different, you knew better, you'd heard this before, you'd seen it all. know thyself: a hurricane is auto-cataleptic chaos while civilization is predicated on order: yes, indeed, they were warned: a radio personality pleaded with his listeners. You're going to think I'm stone cold crazy, but the birds are gone. I know the powers that be say not to panic. I'm telling you, panic, worry, run. The birds are gone. Get out of town! Now! Don't stay! Leave! Save yourself while you can. Go. . . go . . . go! They should have seen it coming, in so many ways the end, this end, this catastrophe, had been foretold, had been written: it was all the news, the main topic of conversation on every street corner, San Calixto redux, the reason for the last minute phone call to a loved one: this wasn't some vatic pronouncement, some oracular premonition, it was 849 millibars, 25.07 inches of mercury, eye wall data; this was science, apodictic certitude, not supposition or superstition, it was inevitable, concatenary, like your next heartbeat: insatiate nature: the last day of creation: a storm surge of more than 30 feet, winds steady at 135 miles per hours, gusting to more than 180 miles per hour, debris turned into shrapnel: it would require a recast of the Saffir-Simpson Scale: few considered the dam a factor at all: historians later claimed that New Johnstown only started to take the storm seriously when all the Starbucks coffeehouses closed early: the hands of God soon to scour His ancient demesne in salt water, said one evangelist, a doomsday upon us, the penalty for a multitude of sins, He will cleanse us of our disease, sayeth He: most of the atheists headed for higher ground; many others left New Johnstown as well: you watched them scurry in fear; you mocked them: many others remained, the fallout of privilege, machismo, stupidity or penury, victims whether they knew it or not: law enforcement scheduled overtime, issued dictates and publically ordered body bags; animal shelters scrambled to evacuate cats and dogs from the danger zone, windows and doors of houses and businesses were boarded up with plywood, people said hasty good-byes to homes and neighbors, driving off in cars crammed with all they could carry: all men are created equal: the others, the unfortunate and the foolhardy, let's call them the residuums, stayed to ride it out, they held storm parties, took casual stock of their foodstuffs, charged batteries, filled gas tanks, dusted off and tested generators, they laughed with nervous bravado as they remembered the dire, departing words of timorous friends and family: the ten commandments: you weren't stupid, you'd prepared, you had enough to endure a few days of deprivation should it come to that: do you think the rain'll hurt the rhubarb?

The sky turned yellow, then darkened into a fiery orange: before long, the time for waiting or preparing or leaving was over, the one-eyed monster neared, the air thickened, the days shortened, first to cloudy hours and then to rain-filled minutes, 849 millibars, 25.07 inches of mercury on its way, the eye wall data: the residuums, motley, vulnerable witnesses to the evolution, the maturation, of the raindrop: fat umbrella-shaped missiles, freshwater bullets en masse, the opening salvo of the storm, band after band and wave after wave, a relentless aerial assault, softening the defenses in advance of the heavy artillery: thirty two feet per second per second: the front line raindrops fall nearly spherical, harmless in moderation, larger raindrops flatten on the bottom, like hamburger buns, while the thickest raindrops plummet parachute-shaped until fate, gravity, speed and mass conspire in a suicidal splatter: the windows of heaven were opened: the incessant din of raindrops striking, without prejudice, every exposed thing: metal, flesh, wood, wet earth; and then there's that unique sound of water hitting water, the result of bubbles of air oscillating under the water, it alone was enough to cause the residuums to question their decision: water, water and more water fell in fat plops from the sky: the pendant odor of petrichor invaded homes, hideaways and penetralia: man is by nature a political animal: alone and in packs, like a funhouse mirror of normalcy, those who remained in New Johnstown calculated the hours and minutes until the storm would pass, they huddled in hilltop homes and valley condominiums, in gated estates and shotgun shacks, they anesthetized themselves with alcohol, drugs, television, food, prayer and sex, they watched the clouds thicken, the air get heavy, the rain, the rain, so much rain; only time or death could stop the rain; water giveth, water taketh away. . . and the waters prevailed:

God is our refuge and strength, a very present help in trouble. Therefore will not we fear, though the earth be removed, and though the mountains be carried into the midst of the sea.

No one noticed, at least no one later admitted to noticing, or maybe no one who survived noticed, the incipient signs of failure at Three Mile Dam as the one-eyed monster of 894 millibars and 25.07 inches of mercury approached, lashing land and sea with her fury: they didn't imagine the dam would fail: Mt. Olympus: the dam, almost 15 miles away from the city, nestled high among the mountains, a world away, a neglected century-old earthen pile of shrubbery and debris so overgrown most assumed the structure was a natural formation: differential and integral calculus: it was anything but natural: everyone, fleers and residuums alike, expected both rivers, the Little and the Big, to overfill their banks given such a rain, to rise and crest and flood; some even anticipated that the levees would fail en masse, after all, the oversaturated earth would be able to withstand only so much, human engineering had its limits, its breaking point, but few considered the possibility that the dam, a dam so removed, so far up the valley, so distant from the broad, gum-stained, sidewalks of the city, would succumb to that hard, cold rain: man is the measure of all things: few considered the dam at all; for the residents of New Johnstown and its satellites it was like living next to an active volcano, ever omnipresent, they forgot it was there, they took it for granted, it was the background of their backyard, a footnote in their long forgotten history, an ignored legacy: the nearer that spinning eye got to land, 894 millibars and 25.07 inches of mercury, the worse things became, the driving rain began to arrive horizontally, the rivers rose at more than a foot an hour, debris raced downstream from both rivers heading directly into the headwinds and sea surge of the great storm: a seemingly perpetual flux . . . inconceivable rapidity: the circumference of a circle is pi times its diameter: the hardest rain anyone had ever heard, it hit with thwacks and thuds: crescendo and decrescendo: unnerving cloud-bursts, a profane simile, like God flushing His toilet on His creation: at some point, at some tragic moment, during the onslaught of rain and wind the dam just moved away: 20 million tons of lake water broke free: the lake leapt down the valley to meet the eye.

In the end they died by the thousands, in awful ways, alone and in groups, their final frantic seconds of life filled with terror: theirs not to make reply, theirs not to reason why, theirs but to do and die: the sixth extinction: some died with strangers, others hugging loved ones, some died heroes, some died martyrs, some died cowards, some died thieves; each though to die alone: bodies of the dead and the dying swirled with the currents: in the whirlpool of Hell there are no names: a maelstrom of sea-wrack and ruin: the lake was rising an inch every ten minutes: yes, they were warned about the storm, warned of the 849 millibars and 25.07 inches of mercury, eye wall data, but no one warned them that the dam was topping, that as they faced their fears of the ocean moving ashore they should have been watching their backs for the moment when the dam washed away, unleashing a three mile long, sixty feet deep, wall of water with preternatural ferocity down the sleepy valley to meet the great eye head on: at four in the afternoon the lake finally leapt free: the dam unable to withstand the sustained hydraulic force and pressure of the water: the wall was a moving grinder: for those in the valley the first warning was often seeing one's neighbors hysterically fleeing for their lives: splintered and uprooted trees and water and debris beyond description: the northern suburbs of New Johnstown were shaved off, right down to the bare rock: $E = mc^2$: crushed and mangled under the weight of man's folly and neglect: witnessing the unwatchable, thinking the unthinkable: as the wall sped through the valley, the deeper water, slowed by the friction of countless obstructions, caused the upper strata of water and debris to continually crash upon itself, to roll over, like a wave, increasing the destructive power of the wall: hundreds spent the night in hillside trees after watching mangled corpses, big screen televisions and railroad cars eddy around them: entire blocks disappeared in an instant: freight cars, automobiles, houses, human and animal corpses carried by the great wave rushed by: the lake was already on its way to New Johnstown: at one point halfway down the sluice, in the midst of its journey, in the middle of a nameless leafy suburb, at a modest concrete bridge, the lake was momentarily recomposed; the debris, the trees, the rocks, and the lifeless bodies of both man and animal all paused with a great weight against the temporary plug; several hopeful minutes passed before the foundation began to shudder and once again the lake exploded down the valley with greater violence than before, crushing homes like eggshells and picking up locomotives: later estimates put the speed at forty miles per hour: Gutenberg: the scars to the valley would attest to heights of more than

50 feet: it became so loud they couldn't hear their own screams: the valley became a millrace for the former lake: those who survived remembered it appearing like a great fire, the dust rising in advance, a blur, a mist: the black wreck, the death mist: the black death: an expertly timed pincer movement on New Johnstown orchestrated by both God and man, a double envelopment, Scylla and Charybdis come ashore: the sixth extinction.

The noise, that horrific wailing, an other-worldly moaning, psychoacoustics, a mixture of the material and the spiritual, of fear and hope, issued from all directions in wavelengths of varying intensities seeming both human and unnatural in turn: pandemonium: the storm turned some residuums into heroes and drove others insane: you watched in fascination as the storm came ashore; you marveled at its power: some residuums risked their lives to save strangers; others risked their lives and lost them attempting to save their pets or their belongings: The Ninety-Five Theses: crushed beneath what had been their sanctuary: the thunderous howl unleashed by the great one-eyed monster competed with the roar of the mountain lake to confuse and destroy the condemned: the earsplitting crash of glass and brick and timber ripping apart: a clamor so deafening that people could not hear their own thoughts: microscope and telescope: it felt like somebody had stuck a screwdriver in my ears: no possibility of greater violence: singularity: a storm surge of more than 30 feet, winds steady at 135 miles per hours, gusting to more than 180 miles per hour, the debris was turned into shrapnel; just as many perished from blunt trauma as from drowning: sirens and alarms and screams: the data taken from the eye wall read 849 millibars, 25.07 inches of mercury: families parted by the waters: rivers of excrement: an inhuman cacophony: a thirty foot storm surge, one hundred miles wide: the wine-dark sea: the lake and its contents ended the 15 mile swath of destruction at the confluence of the barely recognizable Little and Big rivers just as the storm surge made landfall; this mass assembly of liquid force accompanied by the unrelenting rainfall submerged New Johnstown with a violence unseen in human history, a convergence unique to nature and one, perhaps, never to be repeated: The Big Bang, quantum mechanics and black holes: the debris scaled from the valley ultimately gathering at the bridge in the heart of the city, reforming a makeshift dam, reinforced by the rubbish of man, the dead and the dying: chased from their homes the residuums hastily constructed doubtful redoubts with whatever happened to be at hand, until forced again by the flood waters to retreat and rebuild again and again, seeking refuge where none existed: inundation after inundation: those sworn to serve and protect were not spared: one by one the patrols failed to report, all communications were down: stragglers fell through the front door of every police station and every public building hoping they'd found sanctuary: a violent videogame: residuums waded

107

through the water and braved the winds searching for safety: you were still sure you'd survive, though it was worse than anything you'd ever seen: the water was already up to their knees when the storm surge hit and lifted the entire building off its foundation and carried them all for two hundred yards before they managed to gain purchase on a tangle of motley-looking bushes: helpless, the surge carried them inland before they were unceremoniously deposited in a bramble: *veni, vidi, vici*: they spent twelve hours holding on for their lives: Mother Nature's fluid razzia: it scraped the valley bare, the mountain came to the sea: the levees breached as the eye passed: the levee failures appeared to be God's afterthought: the windows of heaven were opened: the coastal police left stranded in trees due to the storm surge, saved by the butt-ugly bush: the water transforms all, decomposition, impermanence: and the waters prevailed: more horrific than the hundreds of corpses was the incredible number of unaccompanied limbs, begging hideous questions: three-fifths of a human being: a stench worse than death: they were blindsided by debris, victims of blunt trauma delivered by everything from animal carcasses and refrigerators to protruding nails and street signs, they were driven by the waves deep into the earth, force-fed a fatal muddy mixture, others were continually tumbled by debris kept alive for a time before their strength and luck ran out: a storekeeper and his son had closed up their shop on the north side of the city which, despite knee-deep water, had stayed open to assist other residuums prepare for the worst: the storekeeper's son shouted to his father and managed to scale a nearby tree before it was uprooted and his grip was loosened by a blow from a dead dog: the detritus of a consumer civilization: PowerPoint and Excel: families parted by the waters: Ulysses himself navigated no worse: an interminable crescendo: a night of indescribable horrors: a residuum family of wealth and privilege ensconced in their compound, a summer house, high above New Johnstown, an aerie in the exhurbs of the city, impotent witnesses to the dual destruction, watching in dumb horror as the lake races down the mountain: Saint Saens' *Le Déluge* in their heads: they worry about their leader, the head of the household, the breadwinner, trapped somewhere beneath them, somewhere in the waterlogged city, out of reach and out of touch: they try to phone and warn others, try to alert the city, but all circuits are dead: revolution: they watch in horror, safe, except psychologically, destined to survive thanks to the luck of economic exemption, but powerless to help others even if they wanted to; they think of their benefactor somewhere in the dark city, neither alive nor dead, they worry selfishly about a lawless aftermath and their own well-being: unable to tweet or Twitter: as darkness descends, the only light in the city they can make out is the inferno raging from the main bridge; they are too far away to imagine the horror in progress, they would have to conjure the screams for themselves:

the eviscerations of Francis Bacon's works brought to life, brought to death: blood and thunder: a caretaker, living in a modest bungalow just outside the family compound felt in his bones the dam would overtop, not knowing what to do he raced outside in the cyclonic wind and driving rain yelling, warning anyone and everyone that the dam would soon be no more, it couldn't hold up: razor sharp shrapnel, man-made projectiles, shards of obsidian, flint, bronze, iron and steel flew past: upon hearing the roar of the water he raced down the ridge to help rescue an old man who'd fallen trying to escape the approaching tumult; without a thought he pulled the old man from the ground and carried him up the rise of the valley: the eagle has landed: he dragged the old man half way up the valley wall, wedged him in between two strong trees and returned to help others, but it was too late, the scouring wall of water, looking like a moving explosion was upon them, pulverizing everything in its greedy path: their bodies, and so many others, would be found months later buried deep by the wave in hidden muddy graves: most heroes go to early graves: shall we give o'er and drown: you could no longer hear yourself: a robust coexistence in time of fire and water: the fire at the bridge refueled by the rapid current, fresh timber, and punctured chemical drums, by kerosene and gasoline: as the flood waters merged they formed a seething soup, a fetid, vomitous stew of the dead and dying, of animal carcasses, of gasping fish, of limbs, of blood, of urine, of excrement, of gasoline, of wiring, of putrefaction, of unidentifiable fluids, of pulp and other unrecognizable detritus: mid the horror of night eternal—waste and void: a waif, her dress ripped by the currents, borne towards the bridge clinging to a tin roof: she had begged her mother to leave the city, all her friends had left, why couldn't they go: in tears she hugged her two favorite dolls until the winds began to peel off the siding of their apartment: cuneiform: it'll be okay, little one, her mother said, daddy will be home soon, it'll be okay: the water surged like the tide, floating everything; they scrambled up the stairs into the attic, the water rising and rising until their heads bumped against the rafters; they instinctively embraced one another in desperation and valediction: structures ripped from their foundations, natural gas lines severed, the odorless gas waiting for the ineludible spark of life: through an act of God or wind, the roof splintered away and they managed to snare a ride on a passing pile of debris: the sixth extinction: three times the mother and young girl slammed into brick buildings, twice the girl groaned upon the breaking of her bones: arms locked, legs kicking as best they could, they fought off assaults from tree trunks and telephone poles: seized from her mother's tired arms by the strong current, the waif watched her mother scream soundlessly before sinking beneath the grimy water: the young girl, parentless, half-submerged in the slurry, pinned against the burning bridge, a broken arm and a fractured leg,

111

the heat from the flames beginning to sear her skin, one of many shouting in fear of flood and flame, suffocation or immolation: the screams from the bridge led one witness to recall, they reminded me of a lot of flies on flypaper, struggling to get away with no hope and no chance to save them: etiolated by fear or by death: vortices of wind and water: you thought it might never stop: the winds stripped the bark off the trees: the lake leapt down the valley to meet the eye: like the day of Judgment I had seen as a little girl in Bible histories: others were unable to utter a single cry, a single lament: even as the winds died down many of those who retreated into catatonia and other psychoses never returned: twin terrors: hieroglyphics and papyrus: in the city itself tales of too many: tales of survival and assistance, nameless and forgotten: a poor teenage black boy struggling to protect the family valuables from the rising waters and inevitable looters: he told his mother not to worry, he'd be safe: the winds whipped, the lights went out, he lit a candle and bravely tried to read *The Tempest* while the rented shotgun shack seemed to inhale and exhale with every blast of wind: he sneaked quick peeks out the window, afraid the glass might blow in on him, he saw the shadows of unabashed gangs ransacking the abandoned houses of the neighborhood: the devil's weather, he thought: and the waters prevailed: no longer any thought of preserving the meager possessions, he surfed with the surge out the back door: Jesse Owens: he jumped back in the water to save one of the gang members, a huge piebald bag of muscles somehow without the critical skill to swim: the second law of thermodynamics: the modest rented house, 75 years-old if it was a day, might just have made it through the storm and the waters until the levees failed, that's when all was lost: a capitalist protecting his empire and his employees, tells them all to get out, get to safety, leave the building, as the winds begin to explode the large windows of the cafeteria; go where, they know not, but they obey: he climbs the stairs, half-lit by failing emergency lights and a tiny flashlight trying to get to his office to see if the phones lines are still working: it's like the mouth of hell, the roiling clouds and relentless waters engulfing the city he'd help build: all was lost, all gone, swallowed by the sea: the winds were so loud he could no longer hear himself think: unable to contemplate a world he couldn't control, an inconceivable apocalypse, he crouched down in a corner of his office, put his hands over his ears and waited for the inescapable: of nature, yet at war with nature, or nature at war with them: Moore's law: the valley denuded: the sixth extinction: we reap what we sow, sayeth He: they believed they were in charge, that they had tamed nature herself: and the waters prevailed: disaster and deprivation being great equalizers: you saw the dead and the dying: a tempestuous noise of thunder and lightening: a businessman trapped in his office three stories high watches a Pepsi machine float by his window: the final

113

graphic manifestation of the city's demise: loved ones and landscapes lost and gone forever: bloated, open-mouthed corpses tangled amidst barbed wire and swing set chains: the hope and sweat of generations erased from the face of the earth: meaning lost beneath the muddy waters: desperation imposed its own democracy: they should have seen it coming, in so many ways the end, this end, this catastrophe, had been written, it had been foretold: thoughts, plans, memories, destroyed by the might of the physical: every minute of survival leads to the next, each interval pregnant with equal parts hope and despair: you understood then that you weren't any different, that you weren't any better, that you weren't special: terrified pets look stupidly to their owners for protection: the holocaust surely destroyed the rescuers as well: the realization that there was no one coming to save them, that any hope of succor was illusory: there's no morality in a hurricane, only death or survival: you swim for your life: the buildings that refused to fall under the pressures of the water provided refuge for the drowned only, repurposed by the storm into multi-storied crypts of steel and stone: otherwise the master of his world: by turns the electrical systems and telephone systems were rendered useless: insatiate nature: the ravaged trough, a once lush valley: some were dragged from their attics by rushing water, others pinned to the beams, their lungs filling with rank floodwater—struggling to hold their breath one more second: a hurricane is auto-cataleptic chaos while civilization is predicated on order: live long and prosper: everything that was within a quarter mile of the shore was either leveled or destroyed or just consumed by the water: a 40-foot fishing boat was carried half a mile over the seaside streets to rest high between a pair of trees in a city park: most of the buildings downtown imploded, unable to withstand the wind and water: the hurricane was like God and the Devil fighting it out with Godzilla as the referee: Guernica: night fell as the eye finally passed over the city and there was nothing for the survivors to do but pray: it tore through the walls, forming bubbles as it bolted between the paint and the sheetrock; the nails popped, one by one, off the shingles: the water came through the light switches and dropped down toward the sink: a hand momentarily breached the swirling waters, like a silent scream for recognition: you swallowed the slurry, again and again, and coughed out what you could: a civilization engulfed in its own waste, the fallout of a reckless quest for material success: once the wounded realized they might just survive, they sought help: an anguished female doctor tries to keep the non-ambulatory alive while the wounded and dying swim through the doors of the hospital believing they've been saved: an elderly couple reaches city hall, relatively high ground, only to find thousands of others also seeking help: the old man, unnoticed, quietly dies from neglect, age and despair, his squatting corpse left to decompose in clear view; his wife of 60 years closes his eyes for him and a stranger throws a dank towel over his head: humans being barbaric and humane, the spectrum on display: Who will wipe this blood off us? What water is there for us to clean ourselves? Some fled earlier to elevated places of refuge, only to later die in squalor, not the victims of winds or water but the victims of indifference and ineptitude: to go we know not where, to lie in cold obstruction and rot: as if all the laws of nature were aligned in anger: in madness, life survives, the green shoots of a parasite: the salinity of the incoming sea floated the living and the dead, the rich and the poor, the rare and the common, with impartiality: a watery *Walpurgisnacht*: the sixth extinction: trees, if not torn up by the roots, were deprived of their leaves and branches: the elderly clutching talismans attempting to out chant the dying howls of the wind: and in the end your arms tired, you could struggle no longer, you wept a little, and you knew you'd die: the music of the damned: chaotic violent death: it would require a recast of the Saffir-Simpson Scale: San Calixto redux: nature's profundity exacting a toll for man's frivolity: a trauma inflicted on earth itself, an indiscriminate self-laceration; the unholy roar of the engine of destruction.

When it was over, when the destruction was halted, when the violence concluded, the silence longed for by those still with ears to hear was smothered by the horrific, pleading, hopeless screams of the dying trapped by debris or being carried out to sea: dragon-flies feasted on mosquitoes, hovering above the foul

116

mixture of bobbing, bloated bodies; dogs cannibalized one another out of fear and hunger: darkness concealed the extent of the devastation.

And when it was over, when the destruction ceased, when the winds died away, when the rain stopped falling, when the violence ended, the silence longed for by those still with ears to hear was missing, swallowed by the echoic aural memory of what they had experienced: life as they knew it would never return, their destinies no longer manifest.

NO, I'M NOT TOO tired. I couldn't sleep if I tried. And that's not how I want to go out anyway. I don't want the end to be easy. Do you? Now don't get me angry again. I said no. Yes, but there are a lot of stars out, aren't there? No, I'm almost done anyway. There's not much left to say. Now don't be sentimental about it. You're welcome. And to be honest, it's helpful for me too. Don't think I didn't know that was part of your plan all along. I'm onto you. Let me go on. There's not much more. We're getting close to the end, my fellow sufferer. My time, whatever you think that means, has almost run out. There are only a few things left to cover.

Information

We all know that through your little internet we can see a lot of cool stuff like watching a kitten eat peanut butter. Yeah, it's a great little toy. Do you remember what I said earlier about history? Please say that you do, you bone-head. Come on, lie to me at least. Remember, that what we call history is only that which managed to get passed down, that most of our history has been lost for all eternity? Ring a bell? Well thanks to technology in general and your little internet in particular that problem has been solved. Now we have an antithetical issue. We have all the information in the world, forever. But what does this mean? How do we make sense of all this information? In terms of history don't worry. History will always be written by those who come after you. Whether they're on the mark or not should be no concern of yours. What you should concern yourself with, however, is how to navigate through the vast seas of information. And it's not only the quality of the information—the integrity of the source. It's about the information itself. With everything at the tips of your fingers, how do you determine what information is valuable and meaningful for you? Or has information been detached from meaning entirely? I have this nightmarish vision of a future in which everyone on the planet reclines semi-catatonic in their own Lay Z Boy playing video games or staring at porn on huge 3-D screens. That's the kind of seductive and jejune 'information' out there that scares me. My fear is that humans will choose the wrong information. That they'll fixate on the flashy and insubstantial, instead of the grave and the difficult. Don't be like them. You have the power over what kind of information you let into your life. Make it count. Make it work for you. What kind of information will help you live your life? What kind of information will make your life better, happier and more meaningful? I wish I had the answer for you. I really do. Even if I did have an answer I'd only have it for myself. It would only apply to my life, my happiness, and that wouldn't do you any good anyway. You'll just have to find your way by yourself.

Success

Everyone should define their own success. Don't let some goddamned gonif tell you that success is a car or a house or having this or that. Define your own goddamned success. Because, let me tell you, it's all crap anyway. Whether you measure it in possessions, progeny, longevity, sexual conquests, health, whatever, success will always be fleeting and disappointing. We are simply not made for success. We are made to be curious, to strive. So even at the moment of hard won 'success' we find ourselves scouting the next challenge, never stopping to understand that there will always be a next and that the only end to this self-inflicted cycle is death itself. And, I guarantee, you will succeed at death.

Language

As I'm certain even you can tell, I'm an educated man. And, as such, I value the nuance and the power of language. Yes, you smartass, for your information there is nuance to cursing. Prick. Back to language. It goes without saying that others judge you by your speech, though by now you well know how little I care for the opinions of others. Bromides notwithstanding, let's move to more consequential matters. Command of language, in speech and in writing—and I'm not talking about penmanship, here. Does anyone talk of penmanship anymore, I wonder?—is your passport to all the world's wonders. Though thought itself may not precede language (a controversial and abstruse philosophical point that need not be argued here), without a mastery of language we are condemned to mental infantilism. Complex thought requires, nay demands, clarity and precision. Ideas need language to live. Language is the skeleton key to existence; we need only seek the doors. To put it in folksier terms, you don't know what you know until you can put it into words. Master language and you will know yourself. That's pretty powerful stuff born of tiny linked letters, isn't it?

And here's a little bonus: as long as you are curious and able to think with clarity life will hold meaning.

One more thing about language that you might find of use is that learning foreign languages is not only the key to understanding foreign cultures, but by mastering foreign languages your own neural networks expand exponentially. Learn a second language and you'll be a better thinker.

Beauty

First of all, don't confuse the beautiful with the sublime. The sublime cannot be discussed. Nothing speaks before the sublime. The sublime is silence. Let's leave it at that. And please don't ever say something has sublime beauty. Ugh. They are different categories altogether. Okay? Okay. Done and done. Beauty can be found anywhere. A mathematical equation, a poem or a sunset may be beautiful. There are beautiful flowers and beautiful clouds. Certainly a woman's face can be beautiful. Textbook definitions of beauty do us a disservice. The idea that a combination of diverse elements in unity leads to beauty does us little good. It's useless didactism. Ultimately, I believe that beauty lives in some netherworld of interaction between observer and observed. And as observers we are highly skilled at finding beauty in things. In fact it seems essential to our well being. We search for beauty, we surround ourselves with beauty, and we covet others' beauty and others' beautiful things. But beauty is fleeting. Beauty is temporary. In the end that may be what we find so attractive. Our relationship with beauty may rest on its temporality, it transience. Perhaps its entire purpose rests on just that: to hold a fleeting flicker of beauty in our big clumsy hands.

Shopping

We all shop. Everybody needs something. It may be an apple or a yacht, but we buy things. And because we are so good at buying things, we buy a lot of unnecessary things. We shop to buy. It's our Zeitgeist. There are those who will tell you that this is the secret, the linchpin, to our entire Ponzi scheme society. They'll tell you if we all stopped shopping our nation would crumble. So, should a national tragedy strike, keep shopping. Should your loved one pass away, buy them an expensive coffin. Lost your job, take a vacation. What would we do without stuff? How would we measure our happiness? How would we measure our success? How would we compete against our neighbors? It can't be all bad, though, can it? I mean, there are an awful lot of people out there who are billionaires. And how can it help us if they keep their money locked away in high security vaults in Switzerland or the Cayman Islands? No, we need these people to shop. We need them to buy things. The world would stop turning otherwise. You know billionaires could spend the rest of their lives just walking around pointing at things, buying everything in sight and they still wouldn't run of money. They would run out of time first. Do you think they made all that money by buying things?

Law and Justice

Once you understand that law and justice are two entirely different things the world will make more sense. It will not make it a better place. But the world will make more sense. It wasn't always thus. The Hittites, for instance, ruled quite well using compensatory justice. There were no loopholes. There were no shades of gray. If you wronged someone, you paid. It was as simple as that. Today we seem to have lost our way.

Today we are ruled by law. We are a nation of laws. That would be all well and good if we were also a nation of justice, if the rules were somehow pegged to justice. But somewhere along the way we divorced the two. Do you really want to live in a country in which justice takes a back seat to the law? Who would we cheer for in movies? What kind of message does that send to our children or to the rest of the world? It's easy to say that it's because we have too many lawyers, but ultimately we have to look at ourselves . . . and our own greed. Contracts today aren't written by lawyers to hold the parties accountable. They are written to allow the parties to escape from what they ostensibly promised. The good attorney is the one who can build in the most escape clauses, the one who can create the greatest obfuscation. Because ultimately untangling such a mess takes time and costs money. And who has the biggest checkbook and the most time—corporations. It's an uneven playing field. And that's just the way they want it. If all men are created equal but under the law some of us have an advantage, how is that being equal and how is that just?

Handedness

This comes down to which one you use to wipe your ass. And apparently, throughout history, more people wiped with their left. Thus for generations we were ridiculed, reformed or worse. Being left-handed myself, I sometimes secretly hope there comes a time when all my sinistral compatriots and I are branded as witches or sorcerers or bad luck charms. We would be shunned and ostracized. This plays nicely into my personality. We would be forced into left-handed ghettoes. We would have our own schools where we cut paper from left-handed notebooks with left-handed scissors. Our corkscrews, should we be permitted wine, would rotate in reverse. We would form our own jai alai and polo teams. We would be banned from fraternizing with righties. Our delusional acquaintances would be out in right field. We would jibe our friends with right-handed compliments. The clumsy among us would have two right feet. Our political spectrum would be narrower. There would be a left way of doing everything. Ah, what a beautiful world it would be!

Bodily Functions

This is where the rubber hits the road, so to speak. It's a great metaphor for human existence. Nowhere else does our self-image clash more with our reality than when we take a well earned shit. From kings to paupers, we all must evacuate our bowels. And it doesn't matter if you can afford to have someone else wipe your ass, you will never escape the daily reminder that you are, no matter what your ego says to the contrary, a disgusting, vile, malodorous animal. This is why prisons and the military are such great equalizers. People who shit together, after a time, no matter who they are or where they come from, are eventually wiped clean, so to speak, of all pretense. Most of the other necessary functions that come with being an animal can be dressed up. Eating daintily, a linen napkin resting on your lap, while a sommelier obsequiously refills your wine glass is civilized. Later that night, alone in your bathroom, amid the gas, grunts and groans of passing a giant, blood-spotted turd, things are somewhat less refined. Look, we are all animals. Do not forget that. And anyone who argues to the contrary should be forced to install festival seating around their toilet to disabuse them of the notion.

Money

Money is a kind of mass psychosis perpetuated by an evil, hidden force . . . maybe by the Federal Reserve or the Rothschilds, if they're still around. Money is not a thing. It's a symbol. And it only means what someone convinces you it means. Imagine visiting a world where the inhabitants trade scraps of paper for huge structures, for animals and food, and even for one another. Okay, you're right. Theoretically, the scraps of paper are backed by something, if only the promise of another imaginary entity. I'll give you that. I'm just saying that one day, if things really get bad—I know, things seem really bad right now. But one day those promises, the backing behind our symbols, may not be worth anything. This isn't some doomsday scenario, some end of the world vision, this is accounting. One day we may hear that an esteemed group of economists have come to the conclusion that all these scraps are, in fact, backed by nothing, that the entire paper system is built on nothing more than a huge misunderstanding. Then what? Oddly enough, my guess is that nothing happens. My guess is that things continue as they have before, that nothing changes. Why, you ask? I can give you three reasons. The first is that I honestly believe that the folks in control, heads of corporations and of state, already know this, are used to it, and are fine with it. Second, it doesn't make any difference at all. If we all got together tomorrow and agreed that termites were valuable, we'd all go out and get as many termites as we could. An object is valuable if we believe it to be valuable. And, third, a general lack of imagination and inertia will maintain the status quo. We'd all just pretend the economists were wrong. What difference would it make?

Hate

Since I spoke of love earlier I would be remiss not to mention hate. Again, like love, I think hate is over- and misused. But I also think most people have little concern about how they use language. Anyway, one of the nice things about hate is that, if used properly, it is a defensive word. I hate you means leave me alone; you are hurting me. I love you means because of my love for you I am willing to be hurt by you. Love gets all tangled up with possessing. Hate, however, is about lack of possession. If you hate something, the last thing

127

on your mind is possessing the thing. Seen in this light, hate isn't such a bad thing really, is it? I hate broccoli. So don't eat it. I love broccoli. You're a moron. As in the preceding example, hate has broader appeal and a wider range of uses. Being defensive isn't necessarily a bad thing. Complete isolation might be bad, though I have my doubts, but defensiveness should be a quality we all understand and embrace. So go ahead. Hate once in a while. You'll be surprised how good it feels.

Humor

Like Schopenhauer said, some show by committing suicide they cannot take a joke. (N.B. His own father's death was thought to be suicide.) And if you can joke about suicide you can joke about anything, right? If you've heard half of what I've been saying you'll know that I think existence is largely horrible and that we delude ourselves that reality is different than it actually is. So what. It isn't of our choosing. No one asked us if we wanted to be a part of this big joke. So we make the best of it. That seems reasonable. And in order to make the best of it we've invented a few things to help us. Art, love and humor are three of our best. Sure, art and love are the biggies. They are the lofty ideals. They get all the attention. They get all the press. But humor is the workhorse of our lives. Humor does all the heavy lifting. You can go days without art or love, but try going more than an hour without a laugh. It isn't a pleasant exercise. Humor can be anywhere, in anything.

Christ, if a guy like Schopenhauer can find it in his own father's death we shouldn't be so affected we can't find it in spades amidst the detritus of our lives. Yes, even here, even now. Hey, here's one of my favorites. How many surrealists does it take to change a light bulb? A fish. Ha. I love that. It gets me every time.

Black and White

Don't worry, I'm not going to lecture you on racism. That's not what this is about. What I mean by black and white is that we tend to see things in this world as opposites, as black or white, as polarities. I think this is a great mistake. One of our worst. It sets up false dynamics that lead to bad assumptions that result in horrendous decisions. If we know anything about this chaotic stew we call life, it's that everything is connected, which implies that black and white share commonalities, that they are simply shades along the same continuum. Polar opposites are rare in the real world. Life is messier than we pretend.

An important corollary to this is patterns. We see patterns everywhere, even where they aren't. We are pattern-creating creatures. This is not an accident. Discerning and revealing patterns has brought us a long way. It's given us mathematics, medicines, physics, music, poetry and on and on. Patterns are important. They have been terribly useful. A change in the land-scape may have meant a predator approaching. Facial recognition allowed us to differentiate between friend

129

and foe. But not everything follows a pattern. All the questions of life cannot be solved by applying patterns. We still haven't found a pattern in pi for Christ's sake. Don't get me wrong, I'm not advocating that we ditch rationality, that we stop using the gifts we've evolved. I'm just saying that not everything can be explained with patterns, so let's be a little judicious in our conclusions. We are an impatient species. The universe employs a different timetable.

Patriotism

I know. Yet another -ism? Hear me out. A hundred years ago perhaps this concept made sense. But when people of every persuasion zoom around the planet at such speeds, and when migration and desegregation of cultures is all but a historical given, do we really need patriotism any longer? Haven't we matured? Aren't we fated to mix and meld until we don't even know where we started? Won't the day come where we'll no longer refer to ourselves as Czech-Pole-Argentinean-Chinese American or Nigerian-Irish-Aussie-Burmese Russian? Won't we inevitably all be mutts one day? Ergo, won't all our countries be adopted homes? Aren't they now? What makes any country so wonderful anyway? Is your country, are its laws and rules, that much better than anyone else's? It's all in the eye of the common biped, isn't it? I mean who the hell can tell the difference between Suriname and Guyana? And for most of us you could throw Turkmenistan, Kazakhstan, Uzbek-

130

istan, Tajikistan and Kyrgyzstan into one great 'stan'—
call it Grandstan and still we wouldn't give a flying fuck.
Yet on the ground, at a micro level, on the borders of
these presumably God forsaken hellholes, you will find
no shortage of idiots willing to fight and die over these
ludicrous names. It doesn't matter that the labels were
forcibly imposed in the first place. No, patriotism
trumps all. No offense, but who in their right mind
wants to rule Kyrgyzstan? Have they ever been
anywhere else? Christ. I guess for most of us it's
harmless to take a little pride in where we are from. It
unifies and helps to strengthen the bonds of
community. I get that. A little sprinkle of patriotism can
spice up the salad. Just remember there's a fine line
between patriotism and nationalism. Take heed.

Holidays

Holiday—it comes from holy day. Religion strikes
again. At least most of our holidays are no longer
religious. Hmmph, only half of the holidays are even
vaguely celebrated for what they are. Mostly we just use
them as a day away from work. Another day we are
forced to socialize with our families, the horror of
which is only slightly tempered by the fact that we are
not at the office. I sure as shit never pondered the
contributions of Lincoln and Washington on Pres-
idents' Day. That's for elementary school children and
historians. Christmas and Hanukkah equal presents.
Thanksgiving means football. Easter is a chocolate

bunny. We try to injure ourselves on the fourth of July and hide from scary children on Halloween. No, thank you. Let me spend my holidays the way I want. I have better things to do with my time off than acquiesce to bastardized religious rituals. Here's how we should spend every holiday: get drunk the holiday eve, sleep in, and then go see a bad movie. Now that's a holiday tradition I would support.

Oprah

She is so perfectly evil that I almost respect her. Almost. If you had the ability to distill all that was wrong with the late 20th and early 21st centuries and create a loud, whining, pharisaic, shape-shifting vessel to embody these ills, you could do no better than Oprah Winfrey. Her pre-school versions of self-help and pseudo-science have lobotomized at least two generations of American women. She has done more to destroy any hope of humanity's progress than anyone else. Armed with little more than a sofa, a variable waistline and an outsized ego, she has single-handedly managed to remove the last vestiges of individual responsibility from millions. That is quite an accomplishment . . . and quite a gift to civilization.

Philosophy

The problem here is that you can't think and do at the same time. All philosophers worth their salt stand outside life. It's an occupational prerequisite. This begs the question whether anything they claim pertains to the real world the rest of us inhabit.

Be that as it may, we have to give them credit for asking the big questions. Remember, too, that for thousands of years philosophy was indistinguishable from scientific inquiry in general. Philosophy was the only game in town. Science sprang from her loins. So, in our day and age, when the field of metaphysics might seem frivolous and academic, let us remind ourselves that they are building on the best traditions of human curiosity, that at the very least they represent the latest link in a long line of catenulate questioners. And, as a species, we can never ask too many questions. If we know one thing it's that the future is unwritten. Philosophers might seem like vestigial tails to us today; tomorrow they may stumble upon the answer to everything.

Space/ETs

Most people couldn't give a rat's ass about space exploration. The general population lost their enthusiasm shortly after we landed on the moon. I'm tired of proselytizing to these morons. Let me put it as simply as I can. Unless we find a way to leave the planet Earth, we all will die here. This I guarantee. Idiots.

I earnestly hope there *are* extraterrestrials out there and that somehow we've pissed them off and they come here and beat the living shit out of the human race. Would that be such a bad thing? Maybe it'll get us off our high horse a little, assuming we aren't entirely eliminated, of course. Maybe it'll take us down a couple pegs. There's another plus to an attack by interstellar beings. All of our petty squabbles, all the infighting and bickering, would dry up the instant some green, antennaed midget in a silver suit threatened us with his ray gun. I can hear the chants of 'Human Beings Unite!' already.

Still, there's the possibility that aliens might be so advanced that they could help us overcome our mistakes and flaws. Peaceful aliens could change our lives for the better. They may have a cure for cancer or for old age. Then again, if they are that evolved they'd probably be smart enough to steer clear of our planet, wouldn't they?

Death

There! Hah. I'm done, finished. The end. Only there is no end, is there? Just like there's no beginning. Alpha and Omega are constructs. It's all simulacra and simulation, fiction, illusion and delusion. Life is metaphysical anosognosia. Should death be any different? Death is without meaning, at least to the dead. It's a nothingness we spend our lives filling with artifice. I hope when I go I don't realize it is happening. But given the bastard I've been I don't expect that'll be the case. I'll tell you, I'm not looking forward to it. Life is all I've known. I'm telling you kid, don't die if you can avoid it.

Has this been at all useful to you? Are we there yet? We don't seem any closer. It did pass the time, yes, I'll give you that. But have you learned anything? Will this help guide your future? Or were you just taking the piss out of me, making an old man talk too much about things that don't really mean a goddamned thing, the impotent, damaged ejaculate of a geriatric? Nothing has changed, has it? Here we sit under the same dark sky adrift in a little red boat, waiting without hope.

DAY ONE – THE DEAD AND THE LIVING

The quivering film iridescent from heating oil, gasoline and raw sewage caught the first flickering light of the new day. The survivors awoke: to a man, to a woman, to a child, to all who lived through the black, moaning night, the diffuse gloaming of dawn brought the realization of survival: the guilt, shock and terror of merely being alive. They observed one another with silent, open mouths, lips trembling from hope and fear, as if they doubted reality itself. Blink by blink they began to reconstruct their environment, their new normal: everything they had ever known shattered, soaked and unrecognizably rising and falling like pond scum as far as the eye could see in all directions. Following the days of roaring wind and rain, the voices of the living and the calls from the birds sounded muffled. All was muted by the storm's din still echoing in their ears.

At the end of exhaustion they found not death, only more exhaustion, greater fatigue, a new weariness.

The dying had died.

The trapped, the stranded and the desperate were legion.

An old man, dry and safe and alone, sat on his haunches in a corner of an office in one of the downtown buildings that had withstood the cataclysm. The windows had been blown out, the furniture rearranged by the wind; contracts, calculations and memos were scattered everywhere. Hours of daylight passed while he sat, unable or unwilling to move; the sounds of the storm still vibrated in the hair cells of his cochleae. A world destroyed, rendered meaningless, he waited for the death that should have come from the storm. He waited. A combination of boredom and cramping muscles finally got him to his feet and once erect he cast a phlegmatic glance at his city underwater and shuffled out the door. Ever so slowly he made his way through the building, past dangling light fixtures, soggy hallways and broken glass before exiting onto an adjoining roof basking in the sunlight, flat and black. He lowered himself against the cowling of a ventilator and looked over an unrecognizable panorama, a vista of water and destruction. Stolid, the warmth of the sun on his face, he closed his eyes and fell asleep.

With clothing still damp and fetid from the storm, a teenage boy paddled through the canyons of New Johnstown in a battered, red, plastic two-person kayak. He used sauce pan lids for paddles. Not quite knowing why, he navigated toward the public library in the vague hope that it was still standing, its treasures somehow miraculously unharmed. But as he pulled his way through the reeking slurry and flotsam, through medical waste and excrement, as he neared his objective, his hopes faded. Most of the buildings in the city were underwater or gone, the grid system no longer evident. He kayaked over submerged parks, schools and parking lots, over liquor stores and streetlights. Despite the stench and the echoes of countless, unseen barking dogs, it was almost peaceful, nice, he thought, the beginning of something new. Just as this thought occurred to him he rounded what used to be Main Street and saw the library. His heart sank. The main public library was underwater, its giant columns completely submerged, only the garland upper façade and the roof were visible. There were tears in his eyes when he turned the kayak around and made his way up what used to be the heart of the city—Claibourne Avenue. All at once his arms seemed weary, the sun seemed hotter, and the water looked menacing. He paddled another half a block and spied a flat roof above the water line. That appears to be as good a resting place as any, he thought.

Steadying the watercraft with care, he gained purchase on the crenelated parapet and pulled himself onto the roof dragging the kayak behind him until it flopped on the black tarred surface with a thud. The old man awoke with the sound.

"Hmmph," came from the old man.

Startled, the kid turned to make out the motionless old man.

"Are you okay?" he asked. "I didn't know anybody was here. I just needed a little break, that's all."

The old man didn't answer.

"Are you hurt?" the kid tried again in a louder voice, walking towards the old man.

"I'm alive," said the old man, stopping the approach of the teenager.

"Yeah, me too. Though I have to tell you that you're the only other person I've seen."

"Bone of my bone, flesh of my flesh," replied the old man.

The Bible? thought the kid. Maybe the storm made him crazy, he thought. I'd better be careful.

"I'm just going to rest here for a little while if you don't mind?" he said. "Then I'll be on my way in my little boat here. I'm just going to lie down and rest a bit, if that's okay?" And he dragged the kayak to the opposite end of the roof.

"Hmmph," said the old man, closing his eyes once more.

The movement of the sun woke them up. The old man's side of the roof eclipsed into shade and the teenager's refuge burned brighter. They both awoke slowly and uncomfortably.

The kid stood up and stretched. He looked over the city, or what was left of the city, before he turned to address the old man.

"I'd better be on my way," he said. "Who knows what's going to happen once it gets dark? It's difficult enough steering this thing around in the daylight."

The old man said nothing. He just stared at the teenager, eyeing him up and down.

"All right, then," said the kid as he picked up his boat. "You're sure that you're okay? You don't need anything? You'll be okay here by yourself?"

The old man blinked twice.

"Okay. Good luck to you," said the kid with a mock wave.

"You'll need water," pronounced the old man.

"You have water?" asked the kid.

"There are a couple of bottles in a refrigerator in the big office on the fifth floor."

"How do you know this?"

"It's my office. It was my office."

"Are you sure?" asked the kid. "Are you sure you can spare some? It's awfully nice of you, but I don't want to take something you'll need. You don't know how long this'll all last."

"Take it."

"You're lying about the water, aren't you? This is some con. You're playing me so I'll go into the building and you can take off with my boat. Nice try."

"Then don't take it."

The old man was so impassive that the kid felt guilty he'd accused him of wanting the kayak. Conscience and manners dictated that he trust the old man.

"Sorry. I apologize. I would like some water. Thank you. Fifth floor you said."

The old man barely nodded.

It was nearly an hour before the kid returned with two bottles of water and a box loaded with other necessities. He took one bottle of water, handed the other to the old man and set the box next to his feet.

"Here, drink this. And I gathered some things you'll probably need. There are some dry blankets and other stuff here to make you more comfortable. Though, you know you could always come with me. There's room enough for two in my boat."

"Thank you," said the old man taking a drink of water.

They both drank quietly; the sun was no longer warming but was still fairly high in the sky. The kid finished his water and motioned if it would be okay to keep the bottle.

"Well, I'm off," said the kid. "You're sure you're okay here by yourself?"

The old man nodded again.

"Thank you, sir . . . for the water."

The kid walked off trying to decide which way to go in all this water. He dropped the bottle in the boat and began to drag it toward the edge of the roof.

"Where are you headed?" asked the old man.

"I don't know," answered the kid turning around. "I really don't know."

"Hmm."

"I should probably go northwest, toward the hills, toward higher ground at least."

"Probably should."

"It might take a while, though. It's slow going what with lids for oars."

"I can imagine."

"Yeah, I'll head northwest. That's what I'll do."

"Hmmph," said the old man.

"That's the best way to go, I suppose."

"Probably."

"Okay, I'm off then. Thanks again," said the kid.

"You know. You could stay here, you know."

"You wouldn't mind?"

"No."

The kid thought about the offer until he felt awkward for thinking about it for so long. He looked at the sky and then the water.

"Maybe I should stay . . . for a little while anyway. It is getting late. And maybe tomorrow you'll change your mind and come with me."

"Doubtful," smiled the old man.

The kid thanked the old man again and dragged the kayak back to its place against the parapet. He then skipped over to the box by the old man and excitedly paraded all the items he'd liberated.

By the time the box was empty, the sun was beginning to set and they could hear the rumblings of each other's empty stomachs.

"Do you think there's any food in your office?"

"No, there's not," answered the old man.

"You don't mind if I go in and take a look around to see if I can find something for us, do you?"

"Suit yourself."

"Do you want to come with me?"

"No, thank you," said the old man.

"May I ask you something? I don't want to pry, but it might come in handy at some point. Can you move?"

"I can. I don't want to."

"Suit yourself," laughed the kid as he ran into the building to look for food.

The old man sat and gazed in the direction of the setting sun. He thought about his family, his wife and his daughter, and wondered if they were alive. They must be, he thought. After all, it was just a storm. He pictured them in the big house above the lake worrying about his safety, fearing for *his* life. They'll be okay, he thought. They'll be fine.

Whistling, his sweatshirt turned into a backpack, the kid returned.

"I scored. It might not be the healthiest, but it's something to fill our stomachs," he said as he unrolled the shirt and revealed an assortment of candy, muffins and potato chips. "Dig in."

"Where did this come from?" asked the old man.

"Oh, I found a couple of vending machines on the third floor, just above the water line, by the way, and grabbed the fire axe and freed our food. Lucky for us, huh?"

143

"You shouldn't have done that. It's criminal," said the old man.

The kid passed a bag of sour cream and vinegar chips to the old man.

"Desperate times call for desperate measures," said the kid, immediately thinking about the gangs looting his neighborhood.

They both ate for a while in stony silence until the teenager spoke.

"We should probably save some of this for later. There's no telling how long it'll be until we're rescued."

The old man sniggered.

"Well if no one comes to rescue us, we'll rescue ourselves," the kid replied.

The light dwindled while the kid built a small lean-to against the air-conditioner casing out of blankets and plastic bags. Stomachs quieted, they divvied up what could be used for makeshift bedding and expressed how tired they were and that sleep would do them both some good.

"Why did you stay?"

"What?"

"Look, I'm not an idiot. I've seen your office. I know expensive clothes when I see them. You certainly had the opportunity to get out of town before this happened. So, why did you stay?"

"I could ask you the same question."

"Yeah, but you can see I'm no rich white guy like you. We don't travel in the same social circles, do we?

144

To you I'm probably just a punk, some lowlife without the smarts to know when to run. Don't be fooled by my age or my clothes. Don't judge me that way. I stayed because I had something to do, something to defend, to protect. I made a promise . . . to myself and others. That's why I stayed."

"Me too," said the old man.

In the dark they could no longer see one another clearly enough to make out facial expressions. It was a mutual disadvantage.

"You don't talk much, do you?"

"What's there to say?"

They fell asleep.

Day Two – The Green Roofs

The faraway hum of helicopters stirred them from their uneasy slumber. The old man slowly opened his eyes and stretched both arms without rising. The kid jumped upright and shouted pointing toward the horizon.

"Helicopters! I can see them."

"Hmmph," responded the old man.

It was a bright, big, crisp, clean, sunny day. The black water sparkled.

The kid bounced over to the old man and sat down talking excitedly.

"Helicopters. What a sight! I have to be honest. I'm relieved. Last night there was a part of me that thought maybe, just maybe, no one was going to come, that the storm, the flood, was part of something bigger, you know, that we were the last ones. Stupid, right?"

"No, not that stupid," said the old man.

"All day yesterday I paddled around and didn't see a single person, not a soul. I didn't even see any dead bodies. I didn't see anyone until I came across you."

"The dead sank, I suspect," said the old man. "The survivors, however many, probably don't share your sense of . . . adventure."

"Look, I know the helicopters are pretty far off, but shouldn't we do something to attract them? Shouldn't we try to get their attention?"

"Probably."

After much discussion they agreed to fashion a large, white arrow out of damask curtains liberated from the office building. Against the flat, jet-black roof, they reasoned, the giant arrow would attract any potential airborne rescuers from afar. The kid at first wanted to spell out help, but the old man said there wasn't enough space on the roof to make it big enough. The kid countered with S.O.S. which made the old man laugh, it being only one letter shorter and hastening to point out that the sole ship in sight was the kid's plastic kayak. The kid countered with an exclamation mark and then an emoticon. Again, the old man laughed and suggested, still laughing, a question mark. In the end they compromised on the big arrow, though the symbol engendered another fifteen minutes of debate over which direction it would point. North prevailed.
When they finished building their sign, they both stared in the direction of the helicopters which in all that time hadn't neared.

"What's that?" asked the kid. "And there's another one."

"What are you going on about?"

Those roofs over there. See. They're all green. They weren't yesterday. Weird."

"Hmmph."

"I don't know about you," said the kid turning his eyes to the old man, "but I have to go to the bathroom."

"So go."

"Where?"

"We are surrounded by a cesspool. Look at that water. You'll be improving it, if anything."

"No thank you. I'll see if I can't find a proper toilet inside. Maybe I can find some more water or something to eat."

"There's no more water," grumbled the old man.
"I'll just take a look around, again, if you don't mind."

When the kid had entered the building, the old man walked over to the edge of the roof unzipped his fly, unfurled his circumcised penis and pissed a steady golden stream into the oily water.

"Kids. Hmmph."

The unrelenting rays of the sun began to melt the tar of the roof forcing the old man to take shelter in the makeshift lean-to. He closed his eyes and started to think about his family and his house in the mountains. Surely they were fine.

The kid returned without water.

"I told you there wasn't anymore."

"You were right. But I did find a toilet, though it wouldn't flush. Well, I was actually afraid to flush it. I thought it might overfill and make a mess."

The old man laughed.

"I couldn't find any other food either. Sorry. But, look, I found a book. And it's dry."

"You like to read," asked the old man.

"It's my favorite thing in the world," answered the kid.

"It used to be my favorite thing too," said the old man. "I used to spend hours and hours with my books. You know, those may have been the happiest times of my life."

"What happened?"

"Oh, life. I guess. Time. Work. Family. Life."

"Here, would you like to read it first. Go ahead."

"No. Thank you, though. You found it."

The kid sat down, squinted a little and opened *The Old Man and the Sea* to page one.

"You want me to tell you what happens?" said the old man.

"Oh, I've read this before," replied the kid. "But it's not about knowing the ending. Is it? It's about how you get there."

The kid's some reader, thought the old man watching him flip page after page. He tried to remember the story and what the kid was reading at that particular moment. After a while he again closed his eyes and thought about his family and wondered whether or not they were thinking about him. They probably assume I'm dead, he thought.

When the kid finished the short book he passed it to the old man. The old man fingered the pages but didn't have the energy to read the words. The kid saw that he wasn't really reading.

"You know those helicopters might not ever see our arrow. It's a beautiful day. How about we get in my boat and see if we can't rescue ourselves?"

"No, thank you," said the old man closing the book. "You go ahead. I think I'll stay here."

"I've got to do something," said the kid. "I can't just sit here all day and hope we get rescued. It's not like you are a scintillating conversationalist."

The old man laughed.

"Are you afraid? Or maybe you'd just prefer to be rescued by a helicopter."

As the old man was about to chuckle again a helicopter buzzed by their rooftop.

They both hopped from out of the lean-to and began waving as the helicopter flew past.

"It's coming back."

It took several minutes before the coast guard helicopter positioned itself safely above them. They could see the pilot and crewmen gesticulating to them. After a few minutes of mime, a long nylon rope dropped from the helicopter and a guard rappelled down to their roof.

The visitor waved off the helicopter, removed his helmet and asked if they were okay.

"We're fine," said the kid. "Well, we're thirsty and

hungry, but we're fine, really."

The rescuer looked at the old man and repeated the question.

"Yes, we're fine."

"Happy to hear that. Happy to hear that," he said. "We saw your arrow. Nice work. Now I have to inform you that we're under strict orders to evacuate only those in critical need." He looked again at the old man. "But if you say you two are okay. Then okay."

He took out his radio.

"Once the helo returns we'll unload some provisions. There's water and MREs. I can't say how long you'll have to stay here. We're only beginning to assess the situation. Are you two alone? Have you seen anyone else?"

"It's just us," answered the kid.

"Okay," he said, turning his attention to the radio. "We'll make sure we leave you with enough for at least a couple of days. Okay."

"Sure," said the kid pausing. "How bad is it?"

"It's bad. It's real bad."

"I mean miles and miles? A lot of dead? How many cities?"

"We don't know yet. Nobody knows yet. We're just trying to save lives right now. I can tell you that almost everything at sea level within 15 miles or so of the coast is underwater. It's incredible. We're finding pockets of survivors, like yourselves, not too many, but some. But we're also seeing bands of looters and criminals. Hell, we've been shot at twice today."

As both the old man and the young kid exchanged glances the helicopter approached and moved into position. The coast guard prepared for his ascent.

"Thank you so much. We truly appreciate all that you're doing. Hey, before you go. Do you see over there, in the distance, those roofs? They're green. Isn't that odd? Do you have any idea what's going on?"

"Turtles," he replied. "For some reason all the turtles are climbing out of the water and basking on the roofs. It's the damnedest thing. You two be careful. We've recorded your coordinates. Someone will be here to assist as soon as practicable. Good luck."

Among much wind and toing and froing, the man was hoisted up and the provisions were lowered down to the roof. They waved as the helicopter was lost to the setting sun.

They both felt energized, rejuvenated, by their visitor and his gifts. They carefully deliberated the amount of food and water and the proper rationing schedule. The old man even began to talk more and actually initiated conversation.

"So tell me. How did you manage to survive this disaster anyway?"

The kid was a little taken aback by the question, not by the question itself, rather the fact that it was unsolicited, but he answered as best he could. He told him about his misguided attempt to protect the family home. He told him how he'd misjudged the power of the storm, the flood, or whatever it was. He told him he hoped his mother wasn't too worried.

"Of course she's worried," said the old man. "She's your mother for Christ's sake."

"What about your family?" asked the kid.
"I presume that they're worried too. But it's different."

"You know what," said the kid. "The storm wasn't even the worst part . . . at least for me."

"What was worse?"

"When things really started to get bad, I mean I could feel the house breathing in and out with every gust of wind, I knew it was only a matter of time before the house would give up. The water was already coming in. It kept getting higher, almost up to my knees. It was bad, but I didn't have time to be afraid, you know. I was reacting to things, trying to live. And then the house just moved. I found myself clinging to a door floating around the remains of what used to be my house. Again, I was just trying to survive and I don't remember being afraid, though maybe I was. Then, right in front of me, I saw him: the meanest, most ruthless thug in my neighborhood. There he was trying to keep his head above water. He didn't look like he could swim. And for all the pain he'd spawned, for all the heartache he'd caused, for all the evil he'd fostered, I wanted to watch him drown. I wanted to watch him die. I really did. A second later I found myself lifting him out of the wreckage and saving the life of that rotten bastard. He couldn't talk. It was like he was in shock. He was coughing up water. We drifted a few minutes before we finally rested among a pile of debris. We looked at each other. The shock started to wear off. And that's when I was *really* afraid. That was the worst part. I thought at that moment he was going to kill me."

"Kill you? He should have thanked you."

"You don't know this guy. Killing is what he does. He doesn't thank people. He takes from people."

"So, he didn't thank you?"

"No, he didn't thank me. But he didn't kill me either. In retrospect I suppose that was his way of saying thanks."

The old man shook his head.

"What about you? How did you manage during the storm? Where were you?"

"Right here. Well, right there. In my office . . .in a corner . . . by myself. That's it. Nothing more to say, I'm sorry to admit. Just luck, I guess, or fate, whatever."

They ate their meals and prepared for another night of camping on the roof. They wished each other pleasant dreams and watched the lights of the helicopters flit like fireflies across the cloudless night.

DAY THREE – THE RETURN OF THE DEAD

"Jesus Christ, kid, you snore like a drunk. I hardly slept at all because of your wheezing and snorting. I almost smacked you."

"Sorry," said the kid. "The sleep of the innocent, I guess."

"Hmmph."

Overnight the winds had changed direction bringing in low clouds from the west. They could no longer see any helicopters in the early morning light, but occasionally they heard one. The winds also brought the smell: a foul odor of excrement, rotting flesh and chemicals. It was relentless and pervasive. It seemed to seep into their clothing. At first the kid thought it was emanating from the old man.

They both tore strips of damask from their arrow and fashioned wrap-around masks to help them breathe without gagging. That was when the kid noticed the first one.

"What is that? I can't. And there's another one.

155

And another. What are they?"

"Christ, they're bodies," said the old man.

On the third day the corpses of New Johnstown returned, raised to the surface by bacterial gas, bobbing like tumefied corks. All of them hideous, bloated, blistered, smelly, the skin loose and dark, stained with blood, some with protruding eyes, most though missing the soft flesh from their face, picked and consumed by crabs and fish. They counted fifteen before they decided to count no more. They looked at one another without speaking. It was as if their world had closed in once again.

"What do you say we load up the provisions, get in the boat and try to get somewhere else?" asked the kid.

"I don't think so. Doesn't seem the wisest thing to do."

"But look at the clouds. It might be days before someone comes for us in this weather, if they come at all. At least this way we're doing something."

"You go ahead. You're young. You'll make it. Go ahead. I'll be fine. I was fine before you came along and I'll be fine when you're gone."

"I can't even eat with this smell and the bodies."

"You won't be able to out paddle the smell and I'm pretty sure you're going to find bodies everywhere, probably more than you've seen this morning, but go ahead . . . send me a postcard and let me know how much fucking better things are out there in the water," sneered the old man.

Defeated, the kid grabbed *The Old Man and the Sea* and sat in a corner. He didn't read, instead he thought about his mother and was kicking himself that he hadn't asked the coast guard to try to get a message out. He was afraid his mother was suffering, that she thought he was dead. He knew how much he meant to her. He was her entire life. He hoped she hadn't given up.

"I can't eat out here," announced the kid. He snatched his allotted morning MRE and carried it into the building next door.

The old man watched him go into *his* building: his beautiful building, his reward to himself for decades of hard work. And now it stood half submerged in crap. He thought about his business or, rather, his former business. He imagined his family fighting over the scraps of his small empire. In every scenario they fought a battle of mutual destruction, all over nothing it seemed to him . . . over money and things. Oddly, he was never able to picture himself there to arbitrate. Maybe that part of my life is over, he thought.

He heard their motor before he saw the boat. For a split second he thought they might be coast guard or national guard or police, but their clothing gave them away. The boat slowly made its way up Claibourne Avenue sidling up to each building, the crew peering into windows, sometimes smashing them with hammers to get a better look inside. The old man realized that they were looters and undoubtedly armed. There was no time to dismantle the lean-to and they would have seen him if he tried to escape so the old man just stood where he was and watched them pick their way up the watery avenue. He hoped the kid hadn't heard their motor.

"Hey old man," one of them yelled. "Do you need any help?"

"No, thank you. I'm managing," he replied.

"How are you managing?" he asked. "Are you alone?"

"Yes. I'm alone."

They pulled up to the parapet and scanned the roof top.

"You're sure you're alone?"

"I'm old, not senile," he yelled. "I think I would know whether or not I was alone. I was alone. Now you're here."

"Pretty funny, old man," he said. "You got anything we might want?"

"What do you want?"

"Everything," he said and they all laughed.

The old man laughed too. One of them was about to climb onto the roof when the leader stopped him.

"Come on, we're wasting time. He's got nothing."

The old man's heart was almost bursting out of his chest thinking that the kid would choose this moment to reappear.

"Okay, old man, we're going now. But we'll see you later, okay?"

Not knowing what to do the old man gave them a feeble wave as they motored away.

He went back to the lean-to and sat down. He couldn't stop his heart from pounding. One of his legs was shaking involuntarily. He was sure he saw a gun on at least two of them. And they said they'd be back. Maybe they would have to leave. Maybe the kayak was the only way out.

A short time later the kid came bounding into the lean-to carrying a load of couch cushions.

"We might as well be as comfortable as possible, right?"

Right away the kid noticed something was amiss.

"What's wrong? You're all red and sweating. Are you feeling sick?"

"Yes, I'm sick, you dumb fuck. I'm sick of everything." shouted the old man.

"Sorry," said the kid sarcastically. "I was just trying to make us a little more comfortable, that's all."

The old man was positively apoplectic.

"Comfortable? We'll never be comfortable here, understand? I'll never be comfortable here. And do you want to know what's making me sick? It's you. That's right. You. You go into my office, *my* building, taking whatever you damn please like it belonged to you. It doesn't. It's mine. Everything in that building is mine. It's not some free buffet that you can pop into whenever you need something. Disaster or no disaster, possessions are possessions. I paid for everything in that building and it belongs to *me*. So do me a favor. If you're going to stay on this roof, the next time you want to go into my building ask, okay? And don't just take whatever you want. Ask, okay? Let's pretend we're still civilized, okay? Let's pretend there's still a fucking rule of fucking law? Would that be too difficult for you?"

Spent, the old man slumped away from the kid who dropped the cushions and left the old man to dwell on his diatribe.

The kid, angered by the old man's ungrateful words, decided to leave. He started to pack up the kayak with everything he'd need for the journey. It was a stupid waste of time to help this old man, he thought. I probably would've been out of this mess already if not for him. Well, screw him. I'm done. He can stay here and rot for all I care.

"Old man," he said. "I'm leaving. May I *please* have my share of the water and MREs? Please," he asked sarcastically.

"Take them."

"Thank you very much," continued the kid. "I know I'm going to regret this, but I will ask you for the last time. Do you want to come along?"

"No, thank you."

"You stubborn old fool. You just want to go by helicopter, don't you?"

The old man almost chuckled.

"Whatever. For what it's worth, thank you for your

rooftop hospitality," he said looking around. "And just so we're clear, I never forgot that this was your building and your stuff. I was trying to help, that's all. I was just trying to help."

"I know," said the old man. "I was a little out of line and I apologize. You have been helpful."

"Are you sure you'll be okay by yourself?"

"Of course," said the old man. "I've got everything a man could want."

The kid laughed and handed the old man the book.

"Thanks," said the old man. "And be careful out there. Not everyone is as nice as I am."

As they both smiled a trembling orange glow from the east caught their attention. An office tower on Farragut Avenue that used to house the local television affiliate was on fire.

"We should go and help," said the kid.

"Help whom? Help what? How?" said the old man.

"We can't sit and watch it burn. Can we?"

"It'll burn to the water line and extinguish itself. What would you do if you were there? Throw a little water on it? Listen, kid, you can't save the world with a little water and a red plastic kayak. Sometimes you've got to let nature take its course."

"Sometimes you've got to fight," said the kid.

"This is not one of those times," replied the old man.

"I'll just go past on my way out."

"But that's the wrong way," said the old man.

"Even so, I should—"

The old man interrupted. "Listen kid, it's already getting late and watching a building burn won't help you get where you want to go. I'll make you a deal. Stay here . . . for now . . . one more night and if, by midday tomorrow we haven't been rescued, I'll get in the goddamned kayak and we'll get out of here together. How's that?"

The kid looked again at the fire and then the old man.

"Deal," he said and they shook hands.

The spectacle and noise of the fire kept them rapt and silent for most of the day. So engrossed were they that neither one of them saw the motorboat approach. When the kid eventually spotted them he knew immediately that they were criminals, looters. They were that same breed of gangster that terrorized his neighborhood. He elbowed the old man and motioned that they should hide.

"They already know I'm here," responded the old man turning his eyes toward the boat. "We had a chat when you were in my building."

"Uh huh," acknowledged the kid.

"Hey, old man, I thought you said you were alone," one of them yelled.

The boat edged closer to the roof.

"I lied," said the old man.

"He lied," laughed the leader. "Old man you got

cojones, I'll give you that. They may be dried up and all saggy and shit, but you got *cojones*," he laughed.

The four men on the boat laughed too. The boat, overloaded with big screen televisions, computers and other electronics, rocked back and forth with their laughter.

"Okay, old man, we've had our fun. Now what else are you lying about?"

"That's it," said the old man. "It's just the two of us. And that's the truth."

The kid started to say something, but the old man stared him down.

"Well, maybe we just come up there and see for ourselves. How's that?"

"I don't think so," said the old man. "I think you should move along."

"Don't think you're calling the shots here, old man. I'm sure you can count. Oh, and a couple of Glocks makes six . . . against two. We're coming up."

"I wouldn't do that if I were you," shouted the old man pulling a thirty-eight from his waistband.

Their eyes got wide. The kid's jaw dropped.

"Relax, old man, relax. Listen, a gun, such determination, all this tells me you're trying to protect something of value . . . and we want it. You're still outnumbered, old man. Just give up the prize and we'll be on our way," reasoned the looter.

"You listen, you fucking punk. Yeah, I'm an old man. But what you don't understand is that gives me an

163

advantage here. You see I don't give a fuck whether I live or die. I've lived my life. I should've died in that storm anyway. I'm done. So, go ahead, try to come up. Odds are you'll kill me and my friend here, but not before I've killed one, maybe two, of you. If it's worth it to you come on. If not, get the fuck out of here."

There was stunned silence. They didn't know how to react. They weren't prepared for a fight. Mounting the parapet facing gunfire was not in their plans.

"Easy, easy, old man, as you can see our vessel here is already at capacity so I'm going to play nice. We'll go now. It'll give you sometime to think about what you said. But this is not over. We'll be back tomorrow. And my advice is that tomorrow you behave a little more respectfully. Let's go."

Before their boat's wake struck against the parapet the old man started shaking, his fear getting the better of him. The kid wanted to hug him as he watched the motorboat race toward the orange glow.

"Why didn't you tell me you had a gun?" asked the kid.

"It's not something that came up in conversation," he said. "I thought it might come in handy. I guess I was right."

Without speaking they understood that they'd be leaving at first light.

DAY FOUR – THE BEGINNING AND THE END

They rose early to a misty morning, another day of helicopters heard but not seen.

They completed loading the kayak with everything they deemed necessary for the journey: water, MREs, tarpaulins, etc. They dismantled their arrow, although the kid wanted to leave it pointing in the direction they were to head. They discussed who would sit in front and who would sit in the rear. The old man practiced getting in and out of the boat. When all the preparations had been made, when they began to drag the kayak towards the parapet wall, the old man spoke up:

"Wait a minute. Come with me."

The kid thought the old man was going to renege on his promise. He couldn't quite figure out whether the old man really wanted to die on this roof or wait for a helicopter rescue that might never arrive. Nevertheless he followed him. They climbed into the office building and made their way to the old man's office. The kid watched the old man look around without saying a word. After a minute or two the old man turned to the kid and said:

"Okay, that's enough, let's go."

Before they exited the building the old man stopped at a cubicle, unclamped a desk light, snapped off one joint of the arm, and removed the light cover and bulb.

"This will make a decent paddle, don't you think?"

He handed it to the kid who read the Waldmann Lighting Co. Valencia E 120V sticker on the improvised paddle. The kid flipped it over in his hands and nodded in agreement. They removed two more and carried them back to the roof.

The red kayak slid gently into the foul brown liquid. The kid got in first and remained standing while he helped the old man into the boat. It took them more than fifteen minutes to coordinate their strokes and move purposefully in a northwesterly direction through the water.

For several blocks, they measured their progress in terms of streets although the grid system was lost deep beneath the surface of the water. They both paddled in relative silence, neither able to vocalize the floating sensation through this new world. They passed through mile after mile of destruction, incapable of determining whether the damage was caused by the storm or looting. They navigated around rotting corpses, both human and animal. The kid kept reminding the old man to rest every so often and to drink plenty of water.

"You need to stay hydrated," he harped.

It was a struggle to put downtown behind them. The current or the tide or the undertow was against them from the start. They eventually reached what used to be a residential neighborhood, now all but gone, and tied up to have lunch. The old man was perspiring and the kid was pensive. They ate quickly.

"Come on, let's get back at it," barked the old man.

"I think a little rest will do you some good," answered the kid.

"We have a long way to go," said the old man.

"This is my neighborhood," said the kid. "It was my neighborhood. That was my block over there."

The old man saw only water. The kid's quarter was gone, wiped off the surface of the earth. Only scattered telephone poles attested to a former civilization.

"I'm sorry," said the old man.

"Yeah. It was a shit hole anyway," said the kid.

The old man laughed. Then the kid laughed. They grabbed their Waldmann's and set off again.

The occasional helicopter could be heard overhead. The kid pointed out where things used to be: the local store used to be over there, the levee walls should be over there, my cousin's house used to be over there.

After an hour or so the old man began to suffer cramping. They rested for a bit, but the old man was getting worse. The kid told him to stop paddling.

"Just sit and try to relax. Let me do all the work. I can get us there. Don't you worry."

The sun began its downward arc. The kid paddled as fast as he could. He thought the old man was going to die on him. That it would be his fault.

The kid tried to keep the old man's spirits up. He talked incessantly. He told bad jokes. He reported they'd be on dry land before they knew it. He narrated his autobiography.

They noticed the water level begin to drop. The tops of roofs appeared. This buoyed the kid and energized his paddling and his conversation.

The old man's arms were feeling better and he was rubbing out the cramping in his legs when they heard a voice.

"Did you hear that?" asked the kid.

"I did," said the old man.

For a second they both thought it was looters and that they should seek a hiding place, but a moment later they heard the weak cries for help. Without asking, the kid paddled in the direction of the sounds.

The cries stopped. They floated silently for a minute or two until the kid spotted a young woman slouched on a rooftop. He yelled to her and she rose.

"I'm here. Thank the good Lord. I'm here," she screamed.

They pulled the kayak up to the house and calmed the weeping woman. She guzzled the water they offered. The old man tore open an MRE and she wolfed it down. They learned her entire family had been washed away. She'd been alone, wailing on her roof, praying for help since. And help had arrived . . . in a red kayak.

The kid pointed out that they couldn't take three in the boat. There wasn't enough room. He said they would leave water and food with her and send help back. The woman began to cry again. The old man offered to trade places with her. She thought for a moment and scrutinized the old man before politely declining and thanking them for all they'd done. She'd be just fine, she said, wiping her cheeks. She'd made it this long. And now she had food and water. But please send help as soon as you can, she said. The old man protested. The kid paddled away and the young woman waved.

"You should've let me take her place," said the old man.

"It wasn't my decision," said the kid. "It was hers."

The old man grabbed the improvised paddle and stroked.

They began to make real progress leaving the city proper and entering the suburbs. Now the hills in the distance were within sight. They kayaked through flooded business parks and landfills. Suddenly, the old man shouted.

"Wait. Over there. Let's head over there."

The old man guided them to a non-descript, half-submerged warehouse.

"That's one of mine," he reported. "Ruined, just like my office."

As they neared, the old man noticed a floating corpse gently bumping against the steel door. The old man made the kid maneuver closer.

"He was the guard," said the old man. "My guard. I don't even know his goddamned name. One of thousands. I don't know a thing about him and he died for stuff, things. My stuff. All for a fucking paycheck with my signature on it."

The old man threw his paddle at the warehouse door.

"Go on if you want," he shouted. "I'm done."

The kid struggled by himself to turn the kayak and regain their course.

Neither spoke for the next hour. The kid half thought the old man had died. It got darker. Lights were discernible in the distance.

The kid spoke first.

"You can give up if you want. You've had your life. I get it. Things suck. Begging your pardon, though, I'll take a different path. You see, this is the beginning of my life, not the end. My journey, whatever that means, has just begun. Storm or no storm. And I know it'll be different. I know the world has changed, but this is my time and I'm not going to spend it feeling sorry for some old man who's decided nothing has value anymore. I'm going to keep going."

"So who's stopping you?" said the old man.

"You'll understand one day, should you live long enough, that is."

"Yeah, live long enough and you're anesthetized by life. I read *All Men Are Mortal*. I understand you now. But with all due respect, things change. Jesus, how things have changed! I get to forge my own way whether you like it or not. And just so we're clear, I think your life still has value, that you still have value, even if you don't."

"Hmmph."

"For instance just imagine what someone like you with all that experience and knowledge could teach someone like me."

The lights were still in the distance. Darkness fell.

"See, we're getting closer," announced the kid.

"We are not," answered the old man. "We're just as far away as we were an hour ago."

"So humor me. We both know you're stuck here and I'm doing all the work. The least you can do is entertain me. So how about it? How about sharing all that meaningless crap you've stored up in that head of yours before it's gone forever? Come on, tell me all about life. What do you think . . . about everything?"

The lights flickered in the distance.

And the old man held forth.

Larry Francis is also the author of *Derrida's Toast*. He and his family split their time—equally— between Chicago and Brittany, France.